Praise for
Six Figures

"A morally challenging novel, an engrossing portrait of a husband and wife left in the wake of a booming economy and an examination of what each is willing to believe about the other in order to stay together. As a social critique, as a study in the evolving dynamics of a couple with young children and as a suspenseful story, *Six Figures* is right on the money."

—*The New York Times Book Review*

"Often funny and always energetic ... The pileup of outrages is almost unbearable, yet each incident resonates with truth. Who hasn't sometimes endured duplicitous colleagues and real estate agents, and longed to flee the emotionally draining demands of family?"   —*Chicago Tribune*

"Fabulously clean, well-lit prose ... Leebron gives us a stereoscopic view of family life—of the nitty-gritty arguing over who filled up the gas tank or changed the baby's diaper last. While we already know it takes a compromise to make a family work, hearing it again from Leebron's intelligently sour tale is well worth the price of admission."

—*Time Out New York*

"As in his 1996 debut novel, *Out West,* Fred G. Leebron's new book visits the darkest corners of his characters' psyches.... These terrifically realistic scenes, in Leebron's beautifully precise writing, are one of the novel's triumphs, but the ambiguity with which Leebron casts the novel is what gives it its greatest strength and honesty."

—*The Atlanta Journal-Constitution*

"Inspired . . . Refreshing . . . Taut prose and intricate nuances in which the author deftly conveys the way anger and resentment can build up and fester in a typical, middle-class American man."   —*Barcelona Review*

"With its fast pace and deft characterizations, this narrative is a gripping one-sitting read. . . . This magnetic tale eludes tidy resolution, providing instead intriguing questions about whether anyone can really trust the ones they love."
                                            —*Publishers Weekly*

"This sharply written novel is populated by seriously flawed individuals, but the compelling immediacy of the story will carry readers regardless of the outcome."   —*Booklist*

"Written in taut prose, *Six Figures* is an intense view of contemporary society—the pressures of a two-career family, the tight scheduling of child care and work, the quest for more money and a bigger home, and the terrible effects of random violence. These people could be any of us."   —Chris Offutt

Six Figures

Six Figures

FRED G. LEEBRON

A HARVEST BOOK
HARCOURT, INC.
San Diego   New York   London

www.harcourt.com

Published by arrangement with Alfred A. Knopf,
a division of Random House, Inc.

Library of Congress Cataloging-in-Publication Data
Leebron, Fred.
Six figures/Fred G. Leebron
p.   cm.—(A Harvest book)
ISBN 0-15-601064-X
1. Suburban life—Fiction.   2. Charlotte (N.C.)—Fiction.   I. Title.
PS3562.E3666 S59 2001
813'.54—dc21   00-048218

Text set in Garamond 3
Printed in the United States of America
First Harvest edition 2001

J I H G F E D C B A

For Kathryn, Cade, and Jacob
and
Barry Wolfman

. . . desires do not split themselves up, there is one desire touching the many things, and it is continuous.

—ROBERT HASS, "NATURAL THEOLOGY"

ACKNOWLEDGMENTS

Many, many thanks to Jennifer Rudolph Walsh, Steve Rinehart, and Ethan Hawke for their early support and encouragement. I'm also grateful to Sonny Mehta, Leyla Aker, Amanda Urban, and the incomparable J.D. Dolan for their diligence, wisdom, and generosity. Thanks as well to Roger Skillings, Andre Bernard, Bruce Tracy, Jay Mandel, Andrew Levy, Don Lee, Debby and Arnie Johnston, Bob Fredrickson, Deb West, Peter Ho Davies, and Geoff Becker for their kindness and tolerance.

Special thanks to Ray and Linda Owens, Barry and Chris Wolfman, Christie Taylor and David Perlmutt, Tommy and Debbie George, Steve and Dawn Ballenger, Henry and Judy Goldman, Wolfman Pizza, the Hodges Taylor Gallery, and Pasta & Provisions for all their help and friendship in Charlotte. Thanks also to the Rhetts of Charleston, South Carolina.

I am especially indebted to Larry Rogers, M.D., for his advice in all matters medical and otherwise.

For support during the writing of this book, thanks to Western Michigan University, Gettysburg College, and the University of North Carolina at Charlotte.

I am most grateful to Kathryn Rhett, for her editorial expertise, patience, and kindness.

Six Figures

Mornings

The line for the polling booths at Charlotte Baptist Church was more than a hundred people long, and Warner Lutz rocked the unsettled baby in his arms while studying the diverse messages posted around Fellowship Hall. *Pray for God to bring the lost and hurting people from your community to himself. Anger is just one letter from Danger.* Every half minute a blue light blinked, and the next person would enter a vacated stall, drawing the curtain closed. At the far end of the auditorium, uniformed children paraded across a stage under a green-and-white banner that said KIDS CAN VOTE, TOO! A handful of Girl Scouts guarded a cardboard ballot box, cheerfully distributing sharpened yellow pencils with pink eraser tips. In Boston, Warner and Megan had voted at a public elementary school, in San Francisco in a row-house garage. The other day a monied pastor had told him that Charlotte liked to view herself as a conservative town who loved her churches on every street corner, and Warner had felt the Jew in him cringe in a kind of fear and the atheist in him vow to do something anarchic about it.

From the start, he and Megan had been torn between blending in and pushing out, but he was feeling increasingly damned if he was going to assume his born-into religion just because everybody around him seemed to put so much stock in theirs. All along the length of the hall his neighbors chatted quietly as they smoothed the minor fault lines in the creases of their business suits or sweater sets, double-checked the coordination of their wristwatches and cuff links or necklaces and earrings. Behind him was Megan in her faded jeans and baby-stained cardigan. She leaned forward and lightly breathed into his ear. "He's asleep."

The little wobbly head was already imprinting an island of drool above Warner's heart. He felt the familiar surge in his throat of gratitude and awe at the unearthly ripeness of the boy's cheeks, the tender narrowness of his neck. How hard he had fought against having him, and now look at the baby and Sophie. Sometimes when he was at the office fielding phone calls from the trustees he understood that his only real reason for living was five o'clock, when he could go home to sit in the beige puddle of their living room and build stacks of blocks to the strains of heartfelt songs from various Disney animated classics. He bent carefully, held his nose close to Daniel's partly open bow of a mouth, and took in the milky breathing.

Megan reached and stroked the baby's hair. "What a cuddlebug." Then she felt Warner's shoulders. "You're still mad? You could wait in the car."

He nodded at the high windows. "It's pouring."

"Everyone should vote," she said. "It's only an hour. You shouldn't resent it so much." She unfolded a pamphlet on bond issues and began to read. "Look, there's education and high-ways and sidewalks, all that stuff we always talk about—"

"—and everyone votes on," he said quietly, "out of ignorance." The baby stirred, and Warner began to sway him back and forth.

"You want me to hold him?"

He shook his head. The boy's bunched knees pressed gently against Warner's rib cage, and his head lolled in the contour of his shoulder. He was six months old, a native Bostonian. Sophie was a Californian. Warner was a Pennsylvanian, and Megan a New Yorker. They'd begun in graduate school, where he was getting a master's in public affairs and she was earning one in art history. She'd said near the end of their first afternoon together, at a graduate student happy hour, that he was the most negative person she'd ever met. He wondered if that were still true. He supposed it was. He rested his head against the baby's head and shut his eyes to a pearled old woman navigating her way into a booth with the aid of a walker and an attendant dressed in white. He wished he had a cell phone so he could check in with the office. He'd denied their request for an electoral day off, and now he himself would be late. Everyone at MORE—he hated the acronym and pushed to get them to answer the phone with M-O-R-E—was from the North or Midwest. Privately, they called themselves nonprofit carpetbaggers and liked to imagine their roles as ideological descendants of the sixties integrationists. But the Metrolina Organization for Resource Exchange was a networker, a facilitator, a broker—all the eighties-nineties tautology that said what you actually did was as close to nothing as doing something could be. Not that he didn't believe in MORE: as its director, he was obligated to. Before his time the organization had helped create the Nonprofit Housing Coalition, the Emergency Food and Drug Delivery System, and the Educational Access Network. It was all paper. He was a technocrat. In Charlotte, who wasn't? But he knew what those other people were making—not that it was only about money, but it was always at least partly about money—and this distinction between them and him made him boil.

"Look where we *could* be," Megan liked to say.

And of course he looked—because he could and he had to, it was part of his job—at what lay under the trapdoor. The poor. The poor poor, the working poor, the criminal poor. The there-but-for-the-grace-of-birth-and-circumstances-go-I poor. The outhouse, crackhouse, madhouse, jailhouse poor. The people-he-thought-he-worked-for-every-day poor. The goddamn-he-was-lucky-he-wasn't-one-of-them poor. Yet he still wanted more. Every morning when he drove Sophie in their shitcan hundred-thousand-plus-mile Honda with the guardrail crease down one side to the private but only $175-a-month preschool and he saw the other parents in their new Volvos and minivans and Suburbans, he wanted more. Every noon when he stood in line at the vegetarian take-out for his cup of soup and can of diet cola while in a nearby café the gray suits and sleek dresses milled between garden salads and poached salmon, he wanted more. And in the evenings when he drew up to the cramped redbrick town-house apartments of Crape Myrtle Hill, having passed the magic dust mansions of the growing rank-and-file rich with their screened-in porches and their two-story great rooms and their eat-in kitchens and their master bedroom baths with built-in saunas, he wanted more. He snuggled the sweet, warm baby draped on his shoulder, and wondered if he would ever understand what enough was, and if so, whether he would recognize when he himself had achieved it. Not twenty feet in front of him was a guy in a sweater more ragged than Warner's, wearing pants with a baggier ass than his. The man turned and offered up a slightly grayer face, halved by unfashionable prescription glasses that sat crookedly on his nose, and showed a set of browning teeth. UnderWarner. He ducked into a polling booth, seemingly holding his breath, and drew the curtain closed.

Daniel pushed at Warner's chest and examined his eyes, his own expression neutral after the abbreviated nap. As they straggled forward in line, Megan reread the pamphlet, her head down, slight shimmers of silver in her hair streaking the shades of brown. Warner loved the gray hair. It made him feel as if they'd endured something together. Now his own glasses bit into the bridge of his nose and he stifled a yelp and snatched at Daniel's tightening fist.

"No," Warner said. "Honey, no." He groped at the tiny wrist and found the pressure point. The baby released the glasses onto Warner's nose. He turned to see if Megan was watching, and his glasses raked across his face, slashing his cheek, and sailed from Daniel's hand, clattering to the hardwood floor. "Daniel! Goddamn—"

Around him was an instant intake of breath, a whispered *oh my* and a murmured *if you please.* He had to remember he was in a church.

"—Let me take him," Megan said, tucking the pamphlet into her back pocket and reaching.

"No, no." He knelt, hiding his red face, still holding the boy, and retrieved the metal frames. He bent them back into shape and fit them on again, trying to ignore a fresh pebbled crack in the lower corner of one of the lenses. "It's all right."

Again, the baby reached for the glasses, clawing at Warner's face. Warner held him out above the floor, the baby giggling and cooing. The underWarner came out from his booth, clutching his neck as if under an invisible burden. Warner felt his own shoulders straighten.

Megan rubbed his back. "You don't mind taking him in with you?"

"Of course not." Maybe for once he'd write in a name or choose Libertarian even though it didn't ultimately mean as much liberty for everybody as he wished it meant. A blue light flashed, and Megan pushed him ahead. In a tight space not unlike an airplane lavatory, an electronic panel glowed yellow under a strip of fluorescent lighting. He saw the name of the Democrat whom socially conscious people like himself were supposed to vote for, and Daniel clawed at him in the metallic closeness. "Okay," he murmured. "Okay." His finger wavered above the choice, and he bent back a switch at what he thought was Libertarian, only to discover that it was the guy he was supposed to choose, the guy with the soft gut and the pursed-lip imperiousness. He tried to flick the switch back but it wouldn't click. He voted the rest of the ticket and then diligently chose positions on the various bond issues. At the last page he saw the word CANCEL and he swiped at the lever and missed as Daniel reached for his face. Now the baby was drooling down his neck and flailing his arms. He hit PROCESS and let it go.

In the car the windows fogged from the rain, the baby began to scream, and Warner kept looking sideways at Megan.

"Should I take him out?" she said. "You think I should take him out, don't you?"

Daniel's roaring shrieked like a chain saw against very hard wood. Along the road Warner could see a filled sign-

board sitting at the edge of a brown churchyard. THE OBJEC-
TIVE OF LOVE IS TO SERVE, NOT WIN.

"Take him out!" Warner shouted.

She climbed into the back, undid the five-point straps,
and pulled the baby from the car seat. Almost immediately, he
stopped crying.

"Whew," Warner said.

"He *needs* another car seat." Megan held the baby close.

Warner swallowed a yawn. They'd both been up most of
the night, attending to a sore ridge of Daniel's circumcision,
where it had somehow recently reattached to a fold and the
doctor, at yesterday's checkup, while looking accusingly at
Warner, had pulled the skin back from itself and then dabbed
on Vaseline. Now whenever the baby peed it stung, and
whenever they changed him it took so long to apply the jelly
that he squirted the wall and soaked himself. It was Warner
who had insisted on the circumcision. "So he can suffer the
way you did?" Megan had asked. No, he'd said. He had a the-
ory that being Jewish was like being a minority, and that a
child who felt this pressure was likely to be a child who grew
up without prejudice, but people rarely believed this. He
wanted to argue that a son should be like his father, that there
shouldn't be any public shower scenes where the difference
would make either uncomfortable, but that point struck him
as pathetically self-referential. As penance those first days, he
had had to tend to the wound, unraveling the blood-crusted
gauze as the baby wailed hysterically and Warner's forehead
broke out in an enormous sweat, and then spool on the fresh
bandage while trying to maintain the wanted shape of the
remaining skin. Undoubtedly he was the cause of the delayed
disfigurement. He wondered what other trials awaited.

"We'll get him a new car seat," he said.

• • •

At Discovery Place on Veterans Day, Sophie and another little girl stood by the rock pool and ran their hands through the water, while Warner and the girl's mother watched over them. A five-year-old in a red dress with a white collar skipped in, her straight blond hair parted and barretted, and hopped up to the edge. She watched the two girls, in their scuffed leggings and generic T-shirts, and held her hands tight behind her back. Two men strolled up, official badges stuck to their chests. One toted a thick camera bag, the other a tripod. Quickly they examined the three girls, then the man with the bag pointed to the five-year-old in the red dress. "Would you like to have your picture taken?"

"Sure."

"Where's your mommy?"

"Upstairs."

"Well, let's go find her and get her permission." He held out his hand and she took it and they hurried together from the room.

Sophie and the other little girl glanced at each other quietly, then went back to touching the water. Warner couldn't look at the mother. At the top of the escalator he could see the perfect little girl, and a woman with expensive hair negotiating with the photographers.

"We could go to the play room," he called to Sophie.

"I want to stay here," she said.

While she picked through the rocks and shells in the pond he tried not to watch the shoot. The little girl in the red dress pretended to feed the mechanical dinosaurs, the little girl in the red dress knelt to examine a live snake, the little girl in the red dress tapped on the glass wall of an aquarium of neon fish. "Be natural," the guy kept telling her. "Have fun." Her mother watched with a mixture of impatience and pride.

The photographers stopped at the rock pool.

"Girls," the one who always talked said.

The two little girls looked up expectantly.

"We need to take a picture or two of the rock pool. Would you mind moving away?"

Sophie and the other little girl started to climb down from the pool.

"Hey," Warner heard himself say. His throat felt clogged, and he was blushing. "You can play where you are, honey," he said.

Sophie stopped.

"Excuse me?" the photographer said, smiling.

"It's still early in the day," Warner said. He heard his voice and tried to erase any fury. "Can't you do this another time?"

"It's just one picture," the guy said. "No big deal."

"Exactly," Warner said. He lowered his voice again. "Do it later."

The photographer looked at his assistant and the little girl's mother and the other mother. They were all staring at Warner as if he'd wriggled out from a crack in the aquarium and was flipping on the floor.

"Well, like you said, sir," the photographer was still smiling, "it is early." He nodded at his people, and they began to move on. The other little girl and her mother left with them.

Warner touched his hands together; they were clenched into fists. He looked at Sophie stroking the water. Beside the aquarium a dinosaur nodded its scaly elongated head as electronic sparks ricocheted in its mouth.

• • •

In the kitchen, as the weekend morning sun slid under the last slat of the venetian blind, he rested an empty coffee cup on the counter, opened the freezer, and brought out the iced bottle of Absolut Citron. He thought he heard something and paused, but there was no one on the stairs. He poured a double and a half, screwed the cap onto the bottle tightly, slipped the bottle back into its place in the freezer, and raised the cup to his lips. The vein in his forehead pulsed. He swirled the vodka with his tongue once in a farewell circuit, and swallowed. Upstairs the baby wailed while his wife quietly argued with their daughter about what to wear to the playground. He wondered what last iota of resistance kept him from drinking directly from the bottle.

"Are you down there?" Megan called over the baby and the child. "I could use a little help."

Wearily he rose. In the cupboard was a single malt, on the refrigerator shelf a chardonnay. He was down there, all right, the flesh around his mouth beginning to numb, his fingertips tingling. He set the cup in the sink. The stairs went up into the havoc and struggle.

"I'm coming," he said, his voice husky.

His daughter waited at the top. "I want to wear a dress." She stamped the carpet with a foot. "Make Mommy let me wear a dress."

He climbed the stairs. "You can wear a dress," he said.

His wife glared from the diaper table, turned back to the baby's flailing legs, looked again. She clapped her hand to her mouth and shook her head. "Warner?"

"Yes," he admitted. He never tried to hide it, but he never confessed it without provocation.

"I thought you were going to take the car in."

"You can take the car in."

She closed the diaper and began snapping shut the onesie.

"I did it last time," he said.

She clutched up the baby and rocked him before he could scream.

Sophie tugged at him. "I'm wearing a dress."

"Absolutely." Under the crib there appeared to be space that no one could see. He got to his knees.

"What's Daddy doing?"

His wife took Sophie's hand and led her from the room.

He was too thick to fit under the crib. He pulled out the activity blanket and tried again. The metal latticework hooked itself the length of the mattress. He poked at the white bedding. "I'm down here," he said. "Down here. Here."

And yet. And yet. He wished he could get up and pour himself into a bed beside Megan, to regain one of those dark early mornings in soundless rooms when it was only the two of them, when he lay awake next to her soft breathing and it all became a little ship that they were on together and he would nose into the mattress as if ducking waves, and he matched her breathing and kept matching it until she woke, vaguely startled, and said, "What is it, honey?" her voice thick with sleep. When they had decided to get married and then got married, he and she had both thought it meant progress, it meant freedom, it meant that now that this issue of whom each of them would be with forever was settled, their forever had no limits. On their honeymoon, they drove down the California coast through a swelling fog to a place that neither of them had ever been, and there was something about the way the fog pressed against the windows and they couldn't see too far ahead and the radio warned of a seventeen-car pileup just behind them and they had a whole week of nothing and nobody they knew in front of them, that their life felt tantalizingly uncertain, and they were squeezing each other's knee as he drove. And he thought they could do anything. Anything they wanted.

She sat in the waiting room of the car dealership, under broad rectangles of fluorescent fixtures, trying to work the slide viewer in the terrible lighting. She couldn't keep herself from going to the glass door and looking at the Honda up on the lift, its hood open, its tires off, and wondering what would it be this time. If the service manager would come and say it was under $200, she could take it. Anything above, and it was almost too horrible to consider. The television blasted a morning talk show featuring country singers and figure skaters. The free coffee tasted like chalk. The good sections of the newspaper had been removed by the staff to a private room where she imagined the mechanics with their feet up, smoking cigarettes. But she could see them working on the cars.

"Ms. Kendall?" The service manager stood behind her. She felt her face going numb. "Could we have a seat?" He gestured to a private corner of the waiting room. She followed him to the facing set of vinyl chairs where they sat like doctor and patient and the man rambled on for a few minutes about the CV joints and the timing belt until she interrupted him with *how much is this going to* and he began what appeared to be a lengthy explanation of all the work they hoped to do and she cut him off again and the manager folded his arms across his chest and looked her up and down, taking measure of her capacity for pain. "With parts and labor," he said, as if there might have been another more expensive way to do it that didn't involve parts and labor but perhaps laser surgery or installation by robot, "we're talking eleven hundred dollars."

"That's awful," she said.

"Ma'am?"

"I mean, is the car worth it?"

"You can't buy a better car for eleven hundred dollars. You only have one hundred and five on this one, and these guys have been known to run as long as two-forty."

Sure, she thought. And everyone would live to be 120. She signed the form, went to the phone beside the coffeepot, and called home to tell Warner.

Work

As Warner walked into MORE's offices on the Tuesday before the board meeting, Monique pulled out a package from under her desk and gave it to him.

"Richard sent it over," she said. Then she gestured to a man in a coat and tie seated with a boxy briefcase at his knee. "I don't believe you two have met yet."

"Welcome to Charlotte!" The coat and tie rose and reached for Warner's hand. "Mike Reynolds of Pfister Holt. We talked a month ago."

"The accountant," Warner said, shifting the package that felt like a framed diploma and officially greeting him.

"Sorry to have taken this long to get around to you, but things are really hopping."

"You bet," Warner said.

"What I usually do is set up shop for a few days right here in the office, and that way if I need anything from you all you're just on hand. This your first audit as a director anywhere? I guess that's kind of exciting."

"It wasn't my budget." Warner smiled. "And for the most part it's not my income or expenses."

"I know, I know. You arrived in September. Well, it won't be pretty."

"It rarely is," Warner said. "Unless you're the American Cancer Society or Toys for Tots." He pointed at the open door of the conference room with its Ethan Allen armchairs, hot and cold water dispenser, and wet bar with refrigerator. "Make yourself at home."

In his own office he shut the door and opened Richard's package. Under a sealed card was a clipping from one of the local papers that Richard had had framed in something that felt like solid brass. MORE GETS TURNAROUND GUY was the piece they'd printed when Warner first arrived in town, detailing how he'd raised ten million dollars in San Francisco and Boston. Warner himself was caught saying that fund-raising was never about money, but about creating partnerships in service to the community. The article went on to underscore MORE's annual operating deficit and its recent decision to totally refurbish its offices. "Money attracts money," Richard insisted. "We had to do this." An accompanying picture showed him and Warner standing side by side, grinning.

"Just a reminder," Richard's attached card said, "of triumphs past and future. Keep at it!"

Warner rewrapped the clipping and put it under his desk. Except for a family photo, his own office was still bare of any personal effects, as if he refused to accept that he had arrived at a place where he'd be staying. Half the people who worked for him had been applying for other jobs ever since they'd started at MORE, and the other half had shaped their positions into sinecures. One of them, Fenton, was quite slowly dying of cancer. There was an office pool, which Fenton himself had initiated, betting on when his ticket would be checked. He'd been here for years and the board had approved the funding of a death policy that would fly him north, to Michigan, to be buried in the family plot with a view of the lake. Warner liked Fenton, and admired how he sucked on hard candies to stifle the bitter cough and returned from medical leaves in a cardigan, button-down shirt, and tie as if to draw a curtain around whichever additional part had been scalloped from him. But the hundred-dollar premium was not an item Warner would have approved: no telling how much longer it would go on, and twelve hundred dollars a year was another twelve hundred dollars that MORE didn't have. Warner could go on and on in this vein—the monthly payment of the office rehabilitation loan, the condo in Raleigh for the two lobbyists with its attendant mortgage and fees, and the annual board retreats at Salter Path, on the beach, in June. "You will *love* the experience," Richard had assured him. "And it's only four thousand dollars for all of us. What's that kind of money when you're talking about a moment of real bonding and understanding?" It's one percent of our entire annual budget, Warner wanted to say. But he kept his mouth shut.

Richard was executive vice president of marketing at one of the top banks. Warner knew which was in acquisition mode, which was led by the more prescient CEO, which was importing the hottest programmers and managers from Atlanta and Tampa. At Crape Myrtle Hill, he was surrounded by the new arrivals, biding their time in three-bedroom, eleven-hundred-dollar-a-month flats that the banks subsidized, while chain builders constructed their monolithic houses in SouthPark or the Arboretum. Over the weekends Warner watched their Range Rovers and sport utility vehicles streaming from the compound in search of country clubs and private schools; each evening when he returned from trailing Sophie around the grounds on her tricycle, he recorded whomever he had met, what and where their positions were. His reputation in Boston was that he could bleed money from a stone, that he was the kind of person who could sell ice-cream sandwiches at a Patriots' game in mid-December. He was the turnaround guy. And he had chosen Charlotte for the same reason everyone he had met had: it was a boomtown and they wanted to boom.

He worked through lunch, sipping at his take-out soup, making phone calls, tweaking program budgets, skimming the update of the on-line project. Toni poked her head in to say that she and Will were off to Raleigh for two days of networking. He made her sit and write out an itinerary of meetings. He'd introduced time sheets back in September, ostensibly as a way of helping them all obtain comp time, but they knew it was because he wanted to assure himself and the board that they worked the hours for which they were being paid. Sometimes he found himself wondering whether he enjoyed being unpopular, if it justified his paranoia. He tried to tell Toni a joke as she finished the itinerary, but she tossed the piece of paper on his desk and waved without looking back as she hobbled on her cane from the office. Richard kept wanting to give her a raise, but Warner would point at the budget and ask from where the money would come. "We give her a lot of flexibility," he once insisted. "That's why she has stayed so long. She could be making three times as much anywhere else." "Why, Warner," Richard had said with a grin, "that would be more than you."

The trustees didn't miss an opportunity to remark on how much he was making, the most they'd ever paid a director, all of 10 percent above the median household income in Charlotte, if you thought along those lines. And Warner did.

When he'd failed to swallow Megan's relativity argument, she had told him, "Don't think in terms of other people." But you couldn't think only in terms of yourself. Not when you watched movies and television shows and noticed even then how much nicer everyone's kitchen was—the butcher-block islands, the two-stack ovens, the South American tile floors, the glass-inlaid cherry-wood cabinetry, the marble counter-tops. Perhaps his negativism was devolving through envy into insanity, but you couldn't fail to see, no matter how much you tried, the quick doubling of the stock market, the decline of mortgage rates, the ascent of salaries of nearly everyone you knew—your mother, your siblings, your college and graduate school classmates—into the land of six figures. But hadn't he chosen nonprofit for service and reasonable hours and his sense of its spirit of the shared endeavor? In San Francisco when he'd first started he saw how wrong he'd been: the foundation treadmill, the grant-seeking rat race. The territoriality. And he understood that he'd made a mistake. At night, in their chummy fourth-story walk-up overlooking the baseball field at Golden Gate Park and its barrage of Saturday BMWs and Porsches, he wrote cover letters and fashioned résumés for openings at investment banks and for-profit consulting firms. Once, only once, did he hear anything, through a former class-mate at one of the firms, who had tried to help and then informed Warner that the firm wasn't certain that he *really* wanted to make money. What do you mean, Warner had nearly screamed into the phone. That's the only reason I'm doing this, is to make money. It's a tough leap to for-profit, the classmate had said. They don't think you have it in you.

Now he sucked up to and manipulated and cajoled any-body who had money, and he tried not to feel dirty or despi-cable because it wasn't for him, it was for a cause. MORE's last

director, a great guy, a wonderful man, had been lousy at
fund-raising, didn't have the stomach for it, and the board had
edged him into another job in another city. In his interview
Warner had talked about first hits and second hits, about nur-
turing partnerships, about bequests and seed money and challenge grants, and he sensed the marvel in their eyes. "I'm not
sure it's what we want," he told Megan on the phone from the
gleaming airport, in a moment of realization that would not
soon enough return and settle in his throat. "But they're going
to give it to us. It's a weird place." "I went home and I told my
wife," Richard purred to him during the long-distance offer
the next day, "that I knew you were the man for the job."

"It's you know who," Monique murmured through the
intercom. "Line one."

"Thank you." Warner hit the line. "Hey, Richard, thanks
for the clipping."

"Any time," Richard said, then he cleared his throat
presidentially. And Warner knew exactly what was coming; it
came around this time all through the week. "So who have
you asked for money today?"

The message on the gallery machine when Megan had finished
feeding Daniel was from the director of Allcomers Pre-School
pleading with her to come get Sophie, that the girl was mis-
erable and had wet herself and had declared that she did not
want to be there. Megan took up Daniel from his activity
blanket, flipped the OPEN sign to CLOSED, and locked up the
gallery. She drove with the window down, trying to inhale any
patience she could drain from the wind.

When she pulled the car into Allcomers' lot, she could
see the curly outline of Sophie's head watching from the win-

dow of the director's office. Megan parked and got out and came around and opened Daniel's door and unbuckled him and said "honey" into his ear and launched him onto her shoulder.

"Just one of those things," Helen whispered to her in the hall. Then Sophie rushed out, pulling Megan's neck down while she was still holding on to Daniel. She forced a smile despite her spasming back.

"Hi, sweetie. We're going to go back to the gallery now, okay?"

She shook her head. "I want to go home."

"Mommy has to work, honey." She pried Sophie from her neck, gathered her hand, reached for the bag of her wet clothes. "Thank you, Helen. I'm sorry."

In the car, surging from Allcomers' lot, Megan said, "So you had a rough time today. Do you want to talk about it?"

"Why did you tell Helen you were sorry?"

"Well." She felt her ears blush while she worked on an answer. "Helen has a lot of work to do, running the school, and she spent all of her time with you. I suppose I should have said just thank you, instead."

"Yes," Sophie said. "Just thank you would have been better."

"Helen said that you were crying a lot. What were you crying about?"

"Jack doesn't like me anymore. I don't like *any* of the potties at Allcomers."

"I see."

"They're always asking if you need to go to the potty and even if you don't sometimes they make you. I *hate* going to the potty at Allcomers." The car turned. "Are we on Providence now?" Megan nodded. "I like Providence. But we're not going

24

home, right, even though Providence is the street we live on. Right?"

"Right," Megan said.

"Why do you and Daddy have to work so much?"

"We don't work that much, honey." At the red light she looked at her daughter, her face without any hardness. "When was the last time you had a poop, Sophie?"

"I don't know." It had been a while, but Megan had lost count. Two days, three days, maybe even four. Sophie didn't let them come in the bathroom with her. She liked the lights on and the door shut. Megan was still looking at her. "Really," she said.

In the gallery Sophie sat in the office and played with Tinkertoys while Daniel napped—a lucky break. Megan dialed Warner and moved with the phone to the front of the gallery where Sophie couldn't hear and filled him in on all the painful details. They had been tracking this for a while, had read up on it in the various parenting books, had tried prune juice and fiber. Now they argued about suppositories and enemas. Sophie rolled out a contraption she'd built, and Megan cut herself off.

"Look at my lawn mower," Sophie said.

"That's excellent," Megan said. "All right," she told Warner. "I want to give it one more chance." She took the phone from her ear. "Honey," she said, "shall we try the potty."

Sophie paused, listening, and then smiled when they both heard the squawking. "I think Daniel's waking up."

He was on the blanket, on his belly, grinning at them. Sometimes he woke up crying and sometimes he woke happy. He rolled over onto his back and Megan picked him up and kissed him.

"When we get home," she said to Sophie. She carried

Daniel to her chair and sat in it with her back to Sophie and began to breast-feed. When they'd brought Daniel home and Sophie had seen her breast-feed, she asked if she could taste, and Megan had later given her a try and was surprised when she'd said she liked it. You're too old, Megan had said. It's for Daniel. But I want some more, Sophie said. Megan shook her head. Sophie didn't want to go to school and she didn't want to go to the potty and she didn't want to grow up and she didn't want to go to college. She wanted to stay home with Mommy and Daddy.

The accountant was sitting cross-legged in Warner's office, the boxy briefcase up on its own chair as if it, too, would speak, explaining after only two days of auditing how he had discovered MORE was another twenty-five thousand dollars in the hole. It had something to do with a grant that MORE had been given to dispense to Metrolina nonprofits as interest-free loans, but no nonprofit had applied—apparently because the existence of the fund had not become known to any of them—and MORE had itself used the money to help deal with its own operating deficit. "That's illegal," the accountant said.

"No kidding." Warner stared at the computer screen where it was his practice to type notes during every meeting in his office. He knew it might seem rude, but he loved the efficiency of it. "What do you think we ought to do?"

"Borrow the money to pay back the fund, and inform the donor." The accountant shifted in his seat. "Bare your neck to him and pray for it to be swift and sure."

"Yeah. Right."

"At least it wasn't on your watch." The accountant rose

and plucked up his briefcase. "You'll need to send me some paperwork on this."

"Of course." Warner shook his hand. "Thanks for the enlightenment."

"Any time."

He sat again in his swivel chair, not letting himself pick up the phone. Richard and all the trustees would want to know. Fenton—who should have known—would need to know. He should call the donor and set up a meeting to tell him in person. He pulled the folder from the right-hand drawer where his predecessor had so precisely left it. It was one of those unusual donations from one of those trusting foundations—a brief letter stipulating what the funds should be used for, with no particular procedural requirements attached. Reports to Due South were to be sent "on occasion." The grant was to be officially anonymous. Twenty-five fucking thousand dollars. Due South had come to MORE with the idea; MORE didn't need to be a bank, but it couldn't refuse the money. What a nightmare. He looked at the phone number, dialed it, held the receiver to his ear. Be honest, he told himself. Do whatever *is* right. Don't lie, don't lie, don't lie.

"I need to come see you," he told the program officer. "To go over some developments with the loan fund."

"Of course." She sounded crisp and assured, almost as if she knew. "How soon should we schedule this?"

He told her that immediately struck him as a pretty good idea.

"Tomorrow, then. At noon. Would you like directions?"

"I have a map," he said. "I look forward to—"

"—Mr. Lutz. Charleston is a complicated place with a great many one-way streets. I'll fax you up directions."

"Of course." Now he was blushing. "Thank you very much."

He called Richard and tried to explain to him in a terse, unexcited fashion what had happened.

"The accountant called me," Richard said mildly. "You know, as a trustee and the president, *I* have ultimate financial responsibility. What are you going to do?"

"Bare my neck, I guess."

"I doubt you'll need to be that direct. Try to talk around it, but of course you must be honest. I do wish I could go with you. But you know my schedule." Richard audibly yawned. "I can't quite believe you failed to pick this up sooner. I thought you were sharper than that."

Warner choked back what he wanted to say. "I appreciate your candor," he said briskly. "I'll talk to you soon."

He paged through the Due South file, the bank statements, the desk calendar. Nine months ago MORE had received the check, deposited it into its regular account, and proceeded to distribute press releases to newspapers that never published them. It was all fuel in the same tank. The books logged the contribution as a fund, and logged the fund balance as the entire account progressively dwindled and that particular line item with it. Quite clearly, in July, there ceased to be a balance. Through the intercom he politely summoned Fenton. His cheeks were drawn and overshaved, his hair too silver. He had on his usual dark cardigan and bright tie.

"I guess you were out most of July," Warner said.

"August, too." Fenton sat where the accountant's briefcase had been. "Why?"

Warner told him.

"Of course I noticed it." He coughed into a handkerchief. "I asked Dan. I'd say his truck was packed. He told me we could just pay it when we had the money and not to worry."

"The accountant seemed pretty pissed off."

"So you going to Charleston?"

"Yup."

"It's a nice town." He folded his handkerchief precisely and tucked it into his shirt pocket. "The way we all sit around here in Charlotte jawing about who makes a lot of money and how they make it, that's the way they sit around in Charleston talking about whose family owned which house and which store before some other family took it over." He laughed self-consciously. "Before my folks moved to Michigan, we came from Charleston. I tried to get back there, but I guess I won't." He coughed into his hand. "Sort of a dream we all had, I guess."

The route south bent away from Columbia before he could really see it, then seemed to rush toward the east. Spanish moss hung like fruit from roadside trees, the mid-November sun wanly illuminating its webbing. Beside a pulled-over bus a dozen men in orange jumpsuits plucked litter while three guards with rifles watched. With each mile he felt more as if he were truly in the South, that Charlotte was too new and concrete and bland. The South wasn't bland, it was extreme in climate, manners, and methods of punishment. It was insidiously solicitous. At a conference last week he'd been introduced to a potential funder from Cincinnati who remarked even before Warner could say a word: "I can tell you're not from around here. I can see your teeth when you smile."

He knew he was right to do this face-to-face, to take what was coming to him in as immediate a manner as possible, to unpack the facts clearly and forcefully, not only to get it over with but also to require the funder to recognize that he and MORE were human. If he'd done it all on the phone, they wouldn't even have considered allowing him the luxury of redemption. He had to put a face on it to gain their empathy. As long as he represented MORE honestly and accurately and as long as he put the organization before himself, he could not fail. At the first sight of palm trees and the hatchwork of bridges arcing over the tangled waterways into the city, he wished that he could pick up MORE and move it entirely to Charleston, that here was a setting as exotic and tropical as he liked to imagine the entire southern half of the country.

Warner parked in front of a stately, cream-colored narrow building that announced its antebellum lineage on a plaque bolted to its door. Black wrought-iron fencing encased a stony cemetery shared with a church. He straightened his glasses and tie, tugged at his tweed sport coat, and stepped into a one-person elevator for the second floor. When its doors opened, a white-haired woman with glinting spectacles reached out her hand to him.

"Mr. Lutz? We've been eagerly awaiting your arrival. I'm Mrs. Baldwin"— he smiled politely through her name—"the secretary. Would you like some tea or coffee?" She pointed to a silver service on a cherry-wood sideboard in the small room. He shook his head and quietly declined. "Miss Horne will see you directly."

She stood in the doorway to her office, an angular woman with short dark hair, wearing a thin gold necklace, a neutral-toned pants outfit. "Warner Lutz," she said, shaking his hand. "Delighted to meet you. Come on in."

She sat in front of a book-lined wall at a large cherry-wood desk, while Warner settled in a wingbacked burgundy leather chair, cleared his throat, and reminded himself not to be intimidated. She was about his age, and—judging from the volumes behind her—of a liberal bent, educated in a familiarly technocratic way. This shouldn't be hard. The only thing new to him was this wasn't a pitch, it was a plea.

"I'm afraid," he said, skipping gratitude for the audience on short notice, mild remarks about the weather, meek pleasantries on how he found the trip and the town, "there's been a misstep that you need to know about, an egregious error on our part that we are capable of correcting. I'm afraid we spent down the nonprofit loan fund ourselves." He stopped to see if she wanted to interject at this point, but she looked at him across her uncluttered massive desk. "We are borrowing money to pay the fund back, and we can either return it to the foundation at once—with interest—or we can administer it in the manner for which it was truly intended. I wanted to come see you and tell you, as I was just informed of this yesterday. It was something that was missed in the transition between directors."

"I see." She studied her desktop blotter, picked at an obtrusive piece of felt. "Could you describe the transition process?"

"We spoke over the phone often. I flew in for two days of meetings."

"Did you review spreadsheets? Did you review the mechanisms of the different grants?"

"We looked a little bit at everything, but I couldn't say we looked at anything with any depth."

"But you were aware of the grant?

"Of course."

"You just weren't aware of the balance."

"Well." He folded his hands on his lap. "Well, I knew

the balance was zero. I'd assumed that it had been appropriately spent."

"And what did Mr. Carruthers say?"

"He said, 'As you see, the balance is zero.' That's all he said." He held her eyes. "I take full responsibility for the error, and I welcome any opportunity Due South could extend for regaining your full trust and support." That was a little stiffer than he'd intended, but it ought to work.

"I see." She nodded and frowned. "Obviously the board here will be displeased. We won't want the money back, yet. We'd like to see if you can do it right."

"Oh, we can do it right."

"I would hope so. You'll need to submit a full report on how this 'misstep' came to pass, and monthly reports on the developing state of both the fund balance and the fund distribution. You can consider this virtually probationary."

"Of course. We're grateful for the opportunity."

"As a member of the Southern Foundation Network," she said matter-of-factly, "we'll feel duty bound to report this to our colleagues in the field."

"We had hoped . . ." Warner felt for the words. "We had hoped that wouldn't be necessary."

"Necessary? It's not necessary." She shook her head. "We're not some backwater antebellum family foundation fresh from the rice fields and the smokehouse. We have a responsibility to a consortium to which we belong. It's duty. That's a distinction you should be familiar with."

"Absolutely." His hands gripped the armrest, and he was pushing up from the damp leather. "I'm sorry I misspoke." He rose, he could not seem to stop himself from rising, even though he knew she should be closing their meeting. He made himself look at her. She took him in without expression, her lips in a line, her face set. She was just doing her job. Still, it had gone worse than even he could have anticipated. "I'm most grateful for your time, and all of us at MORE will work to resolve the situation."

"I'm sure you will."

Awkwardly he offered his hand. She shook it without warmth, and she did not move from her chair. In the outer room Mrs. Baldwin looked at him with what appeared to be disdain. By some miracle the elevator was waiting for him, and he dropped down from the office, red-faced, queasy, stunned, into the humidity of the street. In the car he wished for a cigarette, a drink. The weak sun had made the interior warm, and his face felt overwhelmingly hot in it. So she'd tell all the other foundations. So there would be no more foundation money for MORE. That was it. They were done for. He was done for. God he was hot. He rolled up his window and twisted on the air conditioner. It was nearly Thanksgiving. His shirt under his stupid tweed jacket was soaked. His head was slick with sweat. Boxed air coughed at his face. Charleston passed by, its charming old brick and glass and wrought-iron facades, its tumbledown public housing, its unemployed men sitting atop overturned pails on crumbling street corners, and then he was rising up the highway in the too warm sun, still thinking about a cigarette, how there were no cigarettes and no alcohol; how there'd be no more money coming in, those envelopes that he loved to open with their heavy bond stationery and their deep black ink and their lushly backgrounded checks, from all those foundations that he'd been getting to know in Charlotte and Raleigh and Durham, in Atlanta and Richmond, and how the word would seep out to Washington and New York and Boston. How it had happened on *his* watch, how by missing it for three months he'd made it so much worse. He pried off his tie and swallowed the dusty air. That was the thing, the thing he'd truly overlooked: it was too fucking hot in the South.

Early Sunday morning they sat on a beach blanket on the short lawn in front of their town house, while a bulky Irishman uncoiled a long orange hose from his white van and marched inside with it. She had to explain the equipment to Sophie *and* hold the baby. Warner stared out at empty Crape Myrtle Drive. He was shell-shocked. They were all shell-shocked.

"But why?" Sophie was saying. "Why does he have to clean the carpet? I want it to stay dirty. I like it dirty."

"It's healthier this way," she said tiredly. "Daniel's always putting his mouth to the carpet, and you and Daddy like to wrestle around and play your football game. We're all very close to our carpet, and things that you are close to need to be clean."

"No," Sophie whined. "They *need* to be dirty. They *need* to stay the same. What if it sucks up a toy or a penny? What if he moves Daniel's crib the wrong way and it falls apart like the time it fell on Daddy and he bleeded?"

"Honey, please." From the van the generator groaned and then roared. Sophie began to cry and kick at her. "Warner," she said. "Help me out here."

Mechanically he took the child and pinned her tightly against him. She wailed briefly and fell quiet. It was eight a.m., the only hour they could get the guy to show, and he was charging time and a half. One hundred and fifty bucks. She'd made the appointment without asking him. "I knew you'd say no," she'd said. "But it's unhygienic. And it's depressing." The hardened pools of spilled oatmeal, the dried splats of spat-up sweet potatoes and squash, the nauseating way that the crusted tips of carpet felt against your legs and arms, as if animals had come in at night and shat and peed with an animal joy. He was in a reckless tumble; he could take any line of thought as far down as it would drop. It wasn't self-pity. It wasn't the abyss under the crib after a morning drink. He wanted the chance to be dangerous, to growl and hunt. He hadn't been fired yet. He'd never been fired. But he wanted to be. In graduate school he'd never taken shit from or sucked up to anybody. He'd just done his work, got top grades, but remained—what one professor had termed in a recommendation Warner had inadvertently seen—a social question mark. Which was another reason why he'd probably never got one of those jobs that paid real money. After six nonprofit years of learning to open his mouth and swallow whatever anyone would feed him, he wouldn't mind being a social question mark. A watch-out-for-me-because-I'm-going-to-run-you-over type of guy. He just didn't have the horsepower. He had two kids and a wife who made twenty-five to his thirty-five. One car, forty grand in the bank for an impending house where you didn't have to sleep in the living room and have your home office next to a crib. Or was the forty for a one-year free fall after failing to discover a little twenty-five-thousand-dollar bookkeeping error?

"Warner." She shook him. "Honey, he's done."

"What?" His watch said it wasn't even nine. "One-fifty for *less than an hour*?"

She handed him Daniel and reached in the diaper bag for the checkbook.

"Do you want to have a look, then?" The Irishman grinned from the open door.

"Yeah, we'll have a look," he fought himself from mimicking the accent. With Daniel on his hip he strode in the narrow, short entry hall, too dark and close to inspect. He stood at the precipice of the living room, his mouth falling open. The carpet was so fluffed up and balmy it looked like an immaculate sea or some kind of miraculous soft wax. He put the baby down and felt it. It was just carpet, synthetic, clean, welcoming, like the day they'd moved in. He peeked under the living room table, the magnet for spillage. It was all so beige it was practically white.

"How did you . . ." he said, his voice trailing off as he peered at the shadow beneath the bed. He'd somehow gotten in there, too.

"It's a grand machine," the Irishman said. "You ought to check upstairs." He winked.

Upstairs were so many stains, they were like impressions of a meteor shower. Without baby or child or wife he took long strides up the steps, turned the corner, saw Sophie's room in the morning sunlight. The darkened borders around her bed had been whipped into a creamy froth. He shook his head. There was not even an unevenness to it. Unbelievable. He had never thought beige could look so bright. He turned. Megan was standing there with the children, laced by sun. Heavensent, if you could stomach such a thing.

"What do you think?" she said.

Something was caught in his throat and for a moment he couldn't recognize it, it had been so long. It was a pure, uncynical, apparently unmotivated, idiotic happiness. She kept beaming at him. Sophie danced a jig that in earlier years they called her Happy Step.

"It makes a difference," he said.

On the sidewalk by the closed van he wrote the check,

resisting the impulse to tip. "You do remarkable work," he said.

"I tell you," the Irishman said, and coddled his mustache, "it's a remarkable place. Three years ago I started with one van. Now I have five, and I'm so overbooked I have to subcontract out all the work I can't do, and I'm making twenty percent on that. Anybody who isn't turning a profit in this town isn't working hard enough. How long have you been down then?"

"Just three months," Megan told him.

"I was waiting tables my first three months." He looked behind them at the nearly grand redbrick town house. "You guys are a good sight better off than where I started at. What lines are you in?"

Warner handed him his check while Megan explained. All he could think was paper and art. He wished it were carpet cleaning or asphalt laying or wood work.

"Well," the Irishman said, "of course I wouldn't know how you'd make a killing in your fields." He shook both their hands. "But I'm sure you'll figure it out. Have a nice Sunday." He climbed into his van and drove off, waving and smiling at the children.

It was a nice morning, and they strolled with their children down to the complex's playground of two slides, a baby swing set, kids' swings, and a climbing turtle. He pushed Daniel while she pushed Sophie. Then Sophie climbed out and went over to the kids' swings by herself. It always amazed both of them that she did anything by herself. She was four and a half, and she pumped air like a pro. She was on a steady diet of fibers and mineral oil supplements, probably enough to loosen up a horse. Potty time was a thirty-minute event twice a day, filled with selected storybook readings, sweetness, and encouragement. They were following the doctor's orders. He'd said he suspected that the constipation was hereditary. Warner had to wonder if there was anything positive he had yet passed along to his kids.

His mother called during the fourth quarter of a football game he'd been looking forward all week to watching. He found himself struggling to keep any news from her; if he gave her an inkling of what was going on she would drain the rest from him like water out of an unplugged tub.

"You sound a little down," she said, in that slightly nasal but soothingly familiar voice.

"I'm fine."

"The children?"

"They're fine," he said.

"Should we still come?"

"Whaddyamean?" he barked, then bit hard on his lower lip. Megan was looking encouragingly at him through the pass-through as she occupied the children with two different sets of toys. If there was even a hint of his losing his temper his mother would pick at the scab of the eruption until he'd be practically shrieking at her to let him alone. Why did they always call during the football game? They knew he was watching it! "We want you to come. We're counting on it."

"I talked to your brother the other day. He's going to spend Thanksgiving at the American Embassy in Paris."

"I know. You told me."

"They thought of flying into Charlotte, but they don't want to stay in a hotel."

He clenched his mouth shut.

"*We* don't mind staying at the hotel."

"So when you coming down?" he managed to say calmly; he knew the answer.

"Wednesday before. I don't think we'll make it for dinner, but we'd like to come by and say hello. Is eleven too late? I guess the kids'll be asleep."

"That would be the goal," he said.

"Do you have a minute? Can you talk to your father?"

Through the pass-through against the far wall he could see thousands of people cheering frantically and a boxed clock ticking down in the corner of the screen. "Sure."

"You watching the game?" His voice was thin and gravelly, as if he had just come off of anesthesia from an operation, a familiar state for him. "They have it down there?"

"Of course," Warner said almost proudly. Years and years ago, they'd gone to a few games together, back when the Steelers would win one or three in a season. His father would pick him up from Hebrew School, it would be cold and drizzling, and they'd drive the slow way down to the stadium. They'd sit in damp, dark seats under the concrete stands and watch the visiting team go up by thirty or forty points.

"How's the job?"

Warner winced. Anything he volunteered would subject him to his father's advice. His father had unwillingly retired from advertising and marketing—weren't they the same?—and regarded all that Warner had done, the fund-raising and the program design, within the arena of his own expertise. In an awful way, he was right. "It's fine," Warner said.

"You got money coming in? How are your media contacts? You know, you could give Bill Williams a call—"

"We'll see. I've got a lot of other things on my plate." An expression he absolutely hated.

"Sure, I understand. It's just that Bill Williams—"

"Right, Dad. I know. I've got it written down." No matter where Warner lived, his father knew somebody.

"I did like that new brochure you sent me."

"Thanks." The screen flashed the score, but he was too far away to make it out. "So what have you been up to?"

"Driving ranges," he said.

"Driving ranges?"

"I'm thinking about investing in driving ranges. Some guy started one and now he has twenty. Everybody plays golf. It's a good investment."

"*We* don't play golf, Dad."

"I've got no retirement, no pension, nothing," his father said quietly. "I'm looking for an opportunity. This has a good return rate. I could do it."

"I know you can do it." He wanted to say that they should cash in the house and move to a smaller place, maybe even an apartment. Crape Myrtle Hill had retirees, fragile men and women in their seventies and eighties, who wondered aloud at the mailboxes about how cold it would get this winter and when exactly they should snowbird it to Florida. Some mornings he could see them bending at the knees for their rolled-up newspapers or tottering along after their schnauzers or basset hounds. It was hard for him to believe that his own father was that old. "Well," he murmured. "It does sound like a good idea."

"I knew you'd come around." His father sighed, a mix of self-pity and exhaustion, as if suddenly he himself accepted the improbability of his plan. "I guess you'd better get back to it."

"Yup. Dinner, baths, bedtimes. You know the drill."

"See you soon."

"I love you, Dad. Thanks for calling."

In the living room Daniel was crying, Sophie was laughing, and Megan manufactured a cheerful look. "How is everybody?"

"Driving ranges." He waved his hand. "Don't ask me about it."

Again the kids were in bed. Again the kitchen was clean, the toys in the living room stacked and bagged, the garbage emptied, the phone switched off, the wine poured, the television on. Again it would be Monday tomorrow. Again he sat with a blank yellow legal pad and two fine-point pens. Again she watched him and waited for him to say anything. Again he looked at the television and said nothing. It was the fourth night since Charleston. She knew better than to make him talk about it. She knew that the meeting and his three-month evaluation were tomorrow. Again she sipped at her wine. Again she forced herself to understand or not to understand why it was always more about him than about her or them, that his ten thousand dollars more a year or his maleness or the fact that he had been born the youngest of four children made any misfortune he experienced tip their whole house into the pool of his despair. Over the past few months her gallery hadn't netted as much as she'd been getting paid, and her own head was on the block. Wasn't Milicent wondering aloud just this week whether there should be such a thing as a salaried gallery manager, given the stature of art in Charlotte? "Maybe after this first half year we can work something out that would be more agreeable to both of us," she'd speculated. Megan had smiled and said, "Maybe." Tomorrow she would have to make her own pitch. But it was never about her the way it was so often about him. They'd moved to San Francisco *for him*. They'd moved to Boston *for him*. They'd moved to Charlotte *for him*. She wasn't some vessel, she wasn't an emptiness that someone else had to fill, you didn't have to define her by who she was married to or what her kids were like. It was she who had asked him to marry her in the first place; it was she who had wanted the children. Or did that only mean that she was defining herself by them?

And there he sunk dejectedly with his feet propped on the coffee table, looking glumly at the carpet, pushing the wine down his throat. Come on, she wanted to say. *Come on.* She had to say something.

"That time," she tried, "we were driving to our honeymoon in that fog—"

His head jerked around and then back. She couldn't tell whether he was going to sneer or cry.

"We felt so incredibly clearheaded," she said. "We felt that we could do anything."

"Sometimes." He shook his head, not yet looking at her, which was what he did when he felt ashamed of himself. "I can't even remember what we wanted."

"We wanted kids," she laughed lightly, "which you promptly forgot." She nudged his leg with her toe. "We wanted to be together. We wanted adventure. We got to live in San Francisco and Boston and now here. Maybe here isn't so adventurous, but it could be. I still feel it could be. We're getting to do what we were trained to do. It's not like we're selling real estate."

"Maybe we ought to," he said. "Maybe I'll have to."

"It would make you feel so defeated," she said softly.

"I already do," he said. "Don't you?"

42

She stared at him. What made her feel defeated wasn't what he thought it was; it was how secondary she had at times become. To him. To the children. Wasn't it common wisdom that her generation had been second-class citizens as children to their parents and now were bent on making themselves second-class citizens as parents to their own children?

"No," she said. "Sometimes I feel dull, not as sharp as I want to be. Sometimes I feel patronized or relegated. But I don't feel defeated."

"Well I do," he said.

"You should get over it."

His face pursed to show he had been hurt.

"We both wanted this," she said gently, feeling a twinge of remorse. "You can do this. We both can do this."

She lay her hand on his, and he held it as they drank their wine, their faces close.

"I'm fine," he said. "We'll be fine."

"I know."

"So what you all are telling us," Richard shook his head as he studied the stapled sheets before him, his cheek bulging with a half-eaten doughnut, "is that this was just a mistake, a glitch, a failure in communication."

"I take full responsibility," Warner repeated, looking from one trustee to the next.

"We know, we know." Richard waved him quiet. "Very noble of you. I guess our question really needs to be," he cast sideways glances at his colleagues, "what the heck do we do now?"

"Take the shortfall we owe and the grants we're about to

lose," Nolan Honeycutt grinned nervously, "and we're in the hole for a nice two hundred seventy-five thousand. We'll be toilet paper in a year."

"We could," Alice Polk said while looking at her shoes, "begin to consolidate our position, so to speak."

"Reduce?" Warner asked.

"Cut back," she said.

"If we do that," he said with authority, "we won't ever grow again." He set his hands on the table and leaned forward. "What I think we need is to be more aggressive. To keep our staff. To keep pushing our mission," he privately winced at his own abstractions, "and begin to put some positive pressure on corporate Charlotte to support us. I've been going over the files and I'm stunned to note that none of those guys have been approached. There's our fund-raising opportunity; frankly, outside of the state and federal agencies who are already funding us to the hilt, they're our only opportunity. We have to take it."

"Sure, sure," Richard said nonchalantly. "We can do that. But what about individual donors? We've got some of the wealthiest people *in the world* living in SouthPark, Myers Park, upper Dilworth—they're packed to the gills with money. Why can't we go after them too?"

"We could," Warner nodded, "we can. But individuals would rather support direct-service agencies, and we're not a direct-service agency."

"So what makes you think," Alice asked in that way of hers, "that the corporations will want to fund us?"

"They fund nonservice agencies in Chapel Hill and Raleigh." Warner drew out a folder and distributed a set of photocopies. "USAir, NationsBank, First Union—all those guys—up to five million a year to nonservice, noneducational institutions. We have to make them *want* to be our partners."

"What about the individuals? If you want us to swallow this corporate stuff, you've got to give us some hope for the individuals." Richard raised his eyebrows.

"We'll do a fund-raiser. An event, rather than a direct-mail campaign. That's probably the best way to go."

"Okay. That sounds better. More things that we've got to do, that we've never done before. I like it!" He shuffled his papers. "But listen, I'm sure we can do even better." He looked directly at Warner without smiling. "Like what about those folks down at the synagogue complex? Those folks have a lot of money. You're Jewish. Don't you know how we can tap into those people?"

Warner felt his face blaze. He didn't know what he could say. In an instant he recalled how Richard and Nolan had taken him to breakfast on the morning of his interview day, and how the black waiter had taken his time getting around to their table and Richard had huddled forward and said conspiratorially, "The service is, how shall we put it, *African.*" He had sensed then and in the few days afterward an opening, a chance to walk out through the door that had beckoned. And now here he was. He shook his head and shrugged.

"All right, gentlemen." Richard nodded at him and Fenton. "You all can go."

Warner gathered his notes and pens and made it out of the room before anyone else could speak. In his own office he closed the door and flicked on the computer, pulled up his résumé. No, he'd listed no affiliation, no religion. Maybe he had Jew written all over his face and his every manner. Maybe he was just a whiny Jew. Maybe somehow they had found out.

He didn't hide it. He just didn't believe. He didn't believe in god. He didn't necessarily believe in Israel's right to exist any more than he believed in Utah's or the Vatican's right to exist. He had demanded Daniel's circumcision; that was all. And he fought Christmas with Hanukkah. He glowered at his résumé. Boston hadn't been so terrible. Neither had San Francisco. One place had been all stiff upper lip and the other had been all style. He hadn't been in charge—that was the short-coming—hadn't had his own shop, or whatever the fuck you called it. That damn résumé. In place of the work address he typed his home address and phone number. Should he even keep the new job, or should he act as if he'd relocated on account of his wife? He scrolled to "Executive Director," in boldface like the other job titles, and examined the small dream of it, the small hope. He deleted it.

"Hey, friend." Richard had knocked and entered before Warner had time to turn from the screen. He sat easily in one of the visitor's chairs. "I'm here to share the results." He picked up a photo from Warner's desk, the four of them clowning in pajamas after Daniel had come home. Warner wished he would put the picture down. "We were all very impressed with your work today," he said, looking up from the picture, setting it on the wrong place on the desk. "That corporate pitch idea sounds good. We'll dig into the endowment for operating, and we'll find some funds to front the fund-raiser. A little heavier than our usual style, but that's what we expected from you." He made Warner look him in the eye. "But I have to tell you we're extending your probation another six months."

Warner just stared at him.

"There's the Due South oversight." Richard began to count it out on his hand, already tapped a second finger. "The fact that some of your staff aren't crazy about your management style." A third finger. "The ramifications of your impulsive handling of the Due South issue." The fourth finger. "And your reactive rather than proactive planning." He leaned forward. "You do realize we could have terminated you."

"Today would have been the day."

"We think you're brilliant. We just need to see more focus. You're going to be fine, Warner. We hope to have a very long relationship with you." He rose and cupped a yawn. "Alice will type up the formal evaluation and fax it over to you tomorrow."

"Mail it," Warner said. He stayed in his chair.

"What?"

"I don't want to be standing at the fax machine trying to protect my own confidentiality."

"Of course." He nodded. "Good thinking. Anyway, you read it and, if it suits you, you sign it and mail it back to Alice. Then I'll countersign and we'll file it."

"Excellent." Warner turned back to his screen.

When he was sure that Richard had gone, he checked his watch. Six o'clock. Megan would be coming soon. He wished he could call her first, tell her on the telephone. Then she wouldn't be able to see his face. Now he would have to see hers. He knew what she'd want him to feel: that he wasn't a victim, that it was an adventure, that he'd show them. That he accepted responsibility for what had happened as surely as he'd be responsible for the imminent success. That kind of outcome-oriented vision, in tune with the relentless positivism around them. He knew how to do the damn job; he just had to do it.

When he came out from the building, she was waiting for him, the headlights on, the wipers flicking at the rain. Soft heat blew in the car, and Daniel cooed at him from the back-seat.

"Hi, Daddy," Sophie said, after he'd shut the door and closed them all in that warmth. He turned and looked at her, at the round outline of her cheek. In the dark, she looked healthy. He leaned across and kissed Megan. She backed the car into the street and smiled at him.

"You survived?" she said.

He nodded. "And you?"

"She liked the corporate art idea so much," she said with a forced gaiety, "that she wants me to work more *outside* the office."

"Oh." Through the night rain the lighted trees along Uptown appeared to flash and wink. "That's interesting," he said.

"Yes," she nodded toward Daniel, "that's about all you can say."

"So you're selling out," his mother said, peering over her glass of red wine. The carcass of the turkey lay between them. Upstairs, the children slept. His father snoozed on the sofa in front of the empty television. Megan sat at the head of the table, watching. It seemed like she was trying to decide whether to be tense or not.

He shook his head. "I'm still nonprofit."

"But you're going corporate. You'll be moving in that world. You'll be trying to get money out of it." She gave a tipsy grin. "My corporate son."

"He'll need better clothes," Megan joked.

"Yes," his mother nodded seriously, "and he'll have to shave every day and get a haircut." She reached across and stroked his cheek. "You'll look like a real person!" she said. She wagged her empty glass.

"Mom." He got up and went into the shoebox kitchen, tried not to listen to them in the pass-through. *He's always such a sensitive hothead,* his mother was saying. *I don't know how you put up with him.* He couldn't hear what Megan said. He opened another bottle of red and took it out to the table. His father was staring straight at him through glazed eyes. "You want to lie on the bed?" Warner offered.

He began to push himself from the sofa, an operation that could take a quarter of an hour. "It was just a nap," he said.

"My poor sweet baby," Warner's mother said.

He poured her more wine. His father had made it to the edge of the sofa, sitting up, breathing fast, his neck red and his bald head splotched as if bruised.

"Alan," Warner's mother said. "Maybe we should go."

"No, no." He looked down at the floor, trying to catch his breath. "You guys keep having your party."

"Let's go." His mother took a last gulp of wine and rose from her chair. "This was really nice," she said.

"Thank you," Warner said. He went over to his father and offered his arm. His father stubbornly shook his head.

"We're so glad you could come down," Megan said. "The kids love seeing you guys."

"They're cute kids," Warner's mother said. "Come on, Alan." She heaved her bulging pocketbook over her shoulder and started for the door. "Sorry to leave such a mess."

"That's quite all right," Warner said. He loved Thanksgiving, loved that he was supposed to eat and drink as much as he could stand. Suddenly he felt exhausted. "You'll come by before you leave tomorrow?"

"We'll bring bagels," Warner's father said. His fists whitened and his head and his neck turned deep red as he made one final push from the sofa. He was standing, his belly like ballast. He didn't have any shoes on. "Oh, shit," he said.

"Carry him," Warner's mother needled as she waited at the door.

Warner dug his father's Velcro-strapped sneakers from under the sofa and set them at his feet. Megan opened each sneaker and with his help they guided his father's feet into them. Warner's mother watched, her lips pressed shut. You could tell she wanted to say something, but to everyone's relief she didn't.

"Thank you," Alan said in a tone both humble and bitter.

"All right," Warner's mother said. "Here we go."

"Oh, Ruth." Alan drew out the name. He pointed at a tote bag stuffed with computer printouts and a plastic file box. "Your second office."

"Can you get it?" Ruth asked her son.

Warner started to lift the tote bag. It weighed more than Daniel. "I can't believe you brought this on Thanksgiving," he said.

"She takes it everywhere." Alan wasn't even halfway to the door yet. He was just beginning to get a rhythm to his walk. "Two bags. Everywhere."

"Shut up," Ruth said.

"So what did you think?" she said. She was making him drive, if only to keep him awake.

"They seemed happy. He kept his temper in check. The kids were well behaved."

She nudged him. "You slept through it."

"Some." He yawned. "That was nice."

"Between that and the toilet"— he spent more time in the bathroom than anyone she had ever met or heard of—"I don't think it's right, Alan."

"Ruth." He tried to growl, but she could tell he was too tired. "Don't start."

She looked out the window at the darkened strip malls and gas stations. She'd never seen so many glassy shopping centers holding so many brand-name stores. And that supermarket that Warner and the kids liked, the one that served sushi and had twenty aisles, that looked like a redbrick Taj Mahal.

"He's come a long way," she said.

"Let's *not* go there." Alan warily shook his head.

She glanced at him. Her friends used to tell her that after the three other kids she deserved someone like Warner. As a six-year-old he'd accidentally set a tall bush that grew against the house on fire, and stood there and watched, even though she was inside. That was followed by a few summers of trying overnight camp, when he'd sent them homesick and abusive letters until they came and got him. Years later he was almost suspended from high school for cursing out a teacher, almost suspended from college for a run-in with the dean. And there was a lot of back talk and door slamming in between and beyond, which she didn't need to think about. One professor in graduate school had accused him of waging a vicious smear campaign against another student who was independently wealthy but still had gotten a plum assistantship, and Warner had almost had to withdraw. He was always flying off the handle about not being understood or not getting what he wanted. How he got Megan to marry him, she had no idea. Now he was a director. She couldn't quite believe it.

"Hey." She playfully jabbed Alan's knee and pointed to the lit white dome of the supermarket. "You want to go to that food store?"

He unslumped his shoulders. "Sure!"

The nearly empty lot looked rain slick under the huge lamplights. He seemed to weave or stagger as they walked to the entrance, and she put her arm in his. "You're not too tired?" she said.

"Not for this."

It was past midnight by the time they were settled in their hotel room with the food packed away. He spent his usual half hour on the toilet, groaned from his clothes into his pajamas, sank onto the bed, kissed her good night, and was almost instantly asleep. She turned off the lamp and shut her eyes.

By five o'clock she was rested and wide awake and he was in a full-throated snore enriched by his deviated septum. Within minutes she had herself set up in the bathroom—she sat on the closed toilet seat, with a blue plastic lap desk on top of her, the file box up on the sink, the tote bag at her feet. When they drove to visit the kids she could get work done. When they took their bed-and-breakfast weekends in the country, she could file. She picked out the first billings. She was on her third assistant of the year and her company had acquired its fourth major division. Most weeks, she worked sixty hours. Sometimes she could get it up to seventy or seventy-five. Not bad for a woman of sixty-three. With this last acquisition her salary had jumped thirty percent and the retirement deal was almost enough. She just had to keep going, meet the payroll, keep the auditors happy. If she could hold off another six years she could afford to retire. Not bad for somebody who had never finished college; whose husband hadn't had regular employment in twenty-two years; who never borrowed money from her parents when they were alive or from her kids who now had it (only Warner didn't); who had no professional training. She loved her numbers. She loved making it all add up. She loved that her numbers were made by people and that they made people. Her father had been an accountant.

She sat alone in the tile-and-glass tomb of the bathroom, raking through the numbers, the door so thick that she couldn't even hear her husband, no watch to clock her time. She worked through the latest billing cycle, circled back to fill the holes in payroll, projected forward the quarterly. When she pulled open the door, daylight was seeping into the room. Nine o'clock. He was still snoring. She folded up her office and showered. At nine-thirty she called the kids and told them it was going a little slow. Warner said to just let him sleep. She sat there for a moment and watched him. It was okay for them to let him sleep. It was okay for them to tell her to take it easy on him. It was okay for them to tell her to stop picking at him for what he ate and how he didn't exercise and how much time he spent on the toilet. They didn't have to live with him. They didn't have to wake every morning and wait for somebody who wouldn't even try to get up. They didn't have to try to get out there in the world and see what was going on and enjoy a little bit of life while somebody lagged a block or a mile behind while his feet ached and his blood pressure soared and his gout kicked in. They didn't have to go out to a nice dinner at a nice restaurant with somebody who was only able to dump himself into a pair of Velcro sneakers and a shirt with a popped button, who would keep reaching across the table for the bread and the butter and trying to order the steak or the shellfish because whatever he got to eat was never enough. They didn't have to do the sixty or seventy hour weeks and pre-cook somebody's dinners because if you didn't he'd meander out to the first hoagie shop and have two or three and a root beer. She did love him; he was her best friend, they'd endured forty-three years and raised four wonderful kids and there were not many people who could say that. But the tucking him in and dressing him up, the tracking of his thirteen different prescriptions, the constant watching of his state of being to see if there needed to be yet another operation or procedure where they stuck him in a hospital room for seven to ten to twenty days and blasted him with medicine and hoped for him to work it out while she still did her sixty or seventy hours and visited him at noon and at eight and the kids called and demanded reports and the doctors had to be interrogated and watched so they didn't give him the wrong med or fluid as they had done at least three times before and the fluffing and buffing through the post-hospital recovery period of twelve or thirty or forty-five days with the kids coming in and going out and him trembling between inertia and self-loathing and all kinds of morbid contemplation and keeping the diet right and the weight up and the exercise regimen fair but not too strenuous. And him aging and her aging and the kids aging and their kids aging and everyone getting older and older with time running out until almost no one could move anymore, pinned to the chair with fatigue and desperation, and taxes still to do and bills still to pay and the house falling down with its filled gutters and its leaky furnace and its funny plumbing. A house you can still remember that on the day you moved in forty years ago had that awful odor from the attic and you'd gone up and seen the tiny piles like stalagmites because the toilets hadn't been quite right and the carpenters had used the attic floor as their personal *dumping ground* and you got down on your hands and knees and shoveled up those piles and scrubbed the floor while Alan corralled the kids all eager to see what was going on up in the dark cool room that Mommy had disappeared in and the stains so deep you practically had to soak the floor and still it took a week to ventilate and when you finally mustered the desire to check there were those stains like lily pads all over the floor of your new attic. What a lot of work it all was.

January

*T*hrough the observation window of the shut door at Charlotte Baptist Daycare, Warner could see walls the color of diaper cream, large cell-like cribs, and eight children marooned on their blankets. A redheaded woman clapped beseechingly at a tiny little boy and folded him into sitting while her assistant slopped cereal in a bowl and spooned it to him and Warner kept himself from pressing his face to the glass and waving hello. The yellow mush accumulated on Daniel's face and chin. Suddenly his hand flailed and snatched the spoon and he laughed or screamed, while the thin woman tried to yank it back and the stuff spattered onto the linoleum. The redhead sighed, unfurling a stained wet cloth. She dug and scrubbed at Daniel's mouth and then his nose, until the boy's face was raw and he was sobbing. She picked him up and set him in a crib.

Warner had to turn from the window, and not kick at the door, and not pound at it. In the fridge in the hall he left the noontime milk.

• • •

Over the shrimp her breasts began to leak as if they knew he was crying for her, and she discreetly checked to make sure the pads were in place. It was her third lunch that week at the Bistro. She smiled at the buyer and swallowed a piece of shrimp. It was fine but she missed him, missed the dead moments of noon when they sat and cuddled in the gallery, missed the two daytime feedings that she'd had to drop, missed watching him learn to move with his butt up and his face pitched forward. She rested her fork and mentioned that she could make any of her artists available with a day's notice. The buyer shook his head and asked for four paintings at two thousand each, two already completed and two to evoke water and a lot of green, perhaps touches of gold. He smiled at her as he signed the check.

"You probably think we're awfully obvious," he said.

"Oh no." Megan folded her napkin. "I was thinking Monet."

He grinned. "Good answer."

At the gallery her voice mail had nine messages. Three were from Milicent about the door and the business cards. She wanted to add "Corporate Art." It's not just corporate art, Megan had told her. We don't do only corporate art. Who cares, Milicent had said. The people around here need to know. They'll think it means what I think it means. Let's not take ourselves too seriously, dear. A check-in message from her mother, two messages from artists, two from buyers, and her mother calling again to chat. She sat in the comfortable chair and pried off her low heels. Some of these people loved the idea that the artists could paint start to finish for them. And the money made her artists happy.

She was glancing through the paperwork for the last dozen sales when the trip-bell rang out front. She smoothed her outfit and instinctively checked the square of floor where Daniel would have been playing. In the front room Milicent lingered, minutely straightening a painting. She wore jeans, cowboy boots, and a fleecy sweater. Her light brown hair was curled back behind her ears, showing pearl studs.

"I have tremendous news!" she said.

"What?" Megan couldn't help feeling that she'd created this new ambition. It made her uneasy.

"We're moving uptown."

Megan laughed. "We *are* uptown."

Milicent shook her head. "We're going to rent out space in the atrium of the new bank building. Starting in April!"

Megan considered the stacks of inventory in the back rooms, the clutter of files, the glass sculptures. "We're going to move three blocks?" she said.

"*Uptown.* To a bank! I don't know why I didn't think of this sooner. But this morning, it hit me. Think of the walk-by traffic. They'll have our work in their offices and they'll have it in their homes. It's brilliant. And," she wagged a finger, "there's some kind of child-care deal that you can tie into with the bank. I know how you hate Charlotte Baptist. We all do. You can even run over there on breaks and feed him, if you like."

"You've thought of everything," Megan said.

"You're my girl." Milicent patted her on the back. "I heard from Owens how well your lunch went. Did you know we didn't sell that much in all of January combined last year? Why don't I run out and pick us up a couple of decaf cappuccinos and some scones and we can celebrate?"

"Okay," Megan said, wanting her to leave so she could breathe.

"And don't worry, honey. You won't have to lift a finger on this move."

She slumped into her chair at her desk. This was rich. She should call him and tell him. The phone rang; the white button blinked. It wasn't him; he rarely had time to call anymore. It couldn't be Milicent. Something droned in her ear, and she realized it was the ring of the second line, filling the silence between the purring tones of the first line. She pressed the first light and picked up. "Randolph Whitley," she said. "Can you hold?" She hit hold and answered the second line. "Randolph Whitley," she said. "Can you hold?" Briefly she sat, watching the two lights winking at each other. It was the first time she knew of that both lines had rung at once. She'd have to tell Milicent. It would make her happy. Perhaps the phone would ring all through their cappuccinos and she wouldn't have to say anything; she'd smile apologetically and Milicent would get a phone herself and start coddling the voice on the other line. That could happen. She waited another moment, to see if a line would blink off. They twittered at her. This is good, she told herself. This is what we wanted. We're a success. Now answer the damn phone.

"Sophie." Her teacher sat with her hands folded in her bulging lap as Megan smiled encouragingly at her across the low table in the Allcomers Full Day Family room, wishing she'd get on with it. It was the midyear parent-teacher conference and Mary had already stalled her with too many pleasantries. "Sophie," Mary began again, and Megan widened her smile, "is a couple of beats behind."

"What?" Megan said, the smile dropping from her reddening face, waves of shame and doubt and antipathy crowding instantly in. There hadn't been an incident since before Thanksgiving, and then it was only the one. Who the hell was this woman? "I'm sorry, could you repeat that?"

Mary's finger idly traced a circle on the table. "She's behind," she said firmly. "A couple of steps. In everything. When it's time to get her towel for story hour, she's the last one to do it. When it's time to get her lunch out, I have to tell her about five times. When it's time for pickup, she's the last one out the gate. Always a couple steps. Always has to be reminded. Most of the days she sits on that sofa and stares at the kids playing around her. She can't keep up with them. She's overwhelmed."

"We," Megan said, "we never knew."

"I think you have to consider this year a wash." Mary smiled gently. "Who can say that she shouldn't have been in threes and fours instead of up here in fours and fives. You bring her back here next year, and she'll be more in her element. You hadn't been thinking about kindergarten for her, had you?" Her eyebrows peeked imploringly from above her black-rimmed glasses.

"Well, I . . ." She was reeling, but she had to keep her mouth shut, had to get everything from this woman that she possibly could. "I mean," she said softly, "of course you know Sophie in a whole different way than we do."

"That's exactly right," Mary nodded vigorously, "and she won't be ready. It's nothing to be ashamed of. She has a late birthday—June, right? She could go either way. But she needs time." Mary laughed. "She's one of those kids who has her own internal rhythm. She needs to be in an environment where she can set her own pace, where she won't be rushed. You know, my Martha couldn't tie her shoes until she was nine. She's eleven, and she still can't ride a bike. *I* don't think there's anything wrong with that. If you will love your child for who she is, she won't either."

"So you're saying that Sophie's behind in everything."

"Everything," Mary said.

"Do you think there's anything we should be doing?"

She shook her head. "Let her grow. You know, a lot of these kids, they go right from a day at Allcomers to a play date, on the weekend they'll take gymnastics or swimming or ballet; they're pushed to grow. I don't believe in that. I believe that every child needs to become a person in their own good time." She brushed the lap of her gingham skirt and adjusted a strap of her Birkenstocks. "Our children are special. They're resisting the hurry-up and get-done world we live in. We need to honor that. We need to cherish that."

"But behind?" Megan tried to say it as if it were a word she was just *interested* in exploring.

"Behind." Mary nodded slowly, steadily. "But really, a wonderful child."

"Which skills would you say?"

"Like I've been saying." She smiled, as if explaining to yet another small child. "Social, definitely. Physical, absolutely. These are the ways we see her every day. You know yourself what a struggle potty time is. You know she could take the whole day just getting on her shoes and jacket."

"I thought she seemed pretty happy here—especially since Thanksgiving."

With finality, she shook her big head back and forth. "All the kids have cliqued up. Sophie doesn't have a clique. She doesn't have a set child or group of children that she's paired off with. She sits on that sofa for hours, staring off into space."

And this woman didn't do anything? Apparently that

wasn't her job. The sofa was covered in a nubbed oatmeal fabric, splotched with dark paint stains. Its foam core protruded from one of the cushions, where the zipper had broken free. Threads of clawed upholstery stuck up like strands of hair. That was where Sophie spent her days. Megan cleared her throat.

"The other kids," she tried. "Were they all in the same group last year?"

"No." Mary smiled cheerfully. "Three or four were in one class, five in the other. Ten children, including Sophie, were brand-new to everyone."

"Well," she said. "Well." She rose from the squat little chair. Mary stood, too. She seemed to be reaching for a consolatory hug, and Megan stumbled back from her approach and headed for the door. "I'm glad we've had the opportunity to talk."

"Oh I am too, Megan. Now we'll keep watching her, and if there are any changes, we'll let you know."

"But there's nothing we should be doing?"

"Keep loving her. Like I said, love her for who she is, not for who you wished she'd be."

Megan smiled faintly at the next parents—a woman in earrings, necklace, and some kind of stunning off-red dress, a man in a blue suit, both of whom had heard this last advice— and made her way down the stairs. It was closing in on noon, and the dark-haired assistant teacher was standing guard over Sophie's class in the near playground. Carol had always struck her as bitter and ironic; she'd fallen into teaching at the last minute; she'd rather be working on her music. Megan had always thought it was Mary who knew what she was doing, Mary who had taught at Allcomers for thirteen years, Mary who seemed to have a real passion for the children and for whom, it was obvious to Megan, Sophie had felt affection. Mary who condemned her child as "behind." She stood hidden in the doorway and tried to see Sophie. Strands of children chased in a large circle over the playground, wove their way up and through the treehouse-slide set. She couldn't find Sophie. A group of girls pushed one another on swings; three boys wrestled in a pile. Then she saw what appeared to be a much smaller girl, in a bright red jacket and red plaid skirt, sitting open-legged in the dirt. The girl cupped the dirt in one hand and let it sift down, cupped the dirt in the other hand and let it sift, the children swirling around her, her coat and skirt and ponytail slowly frosting with dirt. "Hi!" the children screamed as they roared past. Or "Don't run over her." Occasionally the girl looked up and smiled but mostly she concentrated on the dirt, the orange-red dirt of Charlotte, the dirt they dug through to add lanes to all the roads and make foundations for all the houses, the dirt they covered with pine needles whenever they tried to grow anything. For the whole time that Megan watched her that poor lonely girl with her sweet ponytail and the tacky red outfit she had chosen for herself played in the dirt. That girl who was behind.

He knew who Mary was. She was the fat bitch with the tree-trunk legs and the barn-sized behind. She wore a lot of denim, and her big fat face had thin judgmental lips and patronizing eyes set behind schoolteacher glasses. Once when he had dropped Sophie at Allcomers Fat Mary had glanced at his dented car and said, "Someone didn't stay awake, did they?" Which was absolutely true: he'd fallen asleep at the wheel at two a.m. on the interstate between his father's heart surgery and Megan's grandmother's funeral. Even so, he hated Fat Mary.

"And you didn't just ram it down her throat?" He tried not to roar at Megan. Upstairs the children slept. What a fantastic refrain. He wished he could say it twenty times a day, not that he didn't love them when they were awake, but god the sugared silence of their sleep! They sat at the table with a half-empty bottle of wine between them.

"I wouldn't have gotten to know exactly what she thinks of our child," Megan said, "unless I kept my mouth shut and asked for it."

Warner tugged angrily at his hair, grabbed at his ear. "Well, now we know. We've got to get her out of there."

"Warner." She shook her head. He seemed as close to tears as to any other reaction. "We have moved around *a lot.* She needs stability. Mary does have some points. What we ought to do is work with Sophie and meet again with Mary, give her a second chance. If she can't say absolutely anything good about Sophie, *then* we have to get her out of there."

"Right," Warner said. He gulped his wine.

"You know, if we pull Sophie from Allcomers, she'll feel the failure."

"You want some ice cream?" he said. "I could use some ice cream."

"It's going to be all right," she said. "Let's not rush anything."

"But we're agreed." He rose from the table, his heart seeming to drop through his bowels, his stomach clenching. She kept looking at him. He couldn't quite believe that there was this, too. That it was January and he had only twelve thousand dollars' worth of corporate pledges. That he'd made one hundred and fifty calls and printed two thousand brochures and sat through four dozen meetings. That Daniel teethed continuously, waking at midnight for two-hour seances of Tylenol and crackers and iced water. That he was on his third cold in four weeks, the tender grooved skin from his nostrils to the apex of his pouty upper lip crusted and red. They'd been getting her clothes on for her and washing her face for her and carrying her lunch bag for her, because of the constant hurry, and now he felt certain that they'd been letting her slide. That it was their fault. Megan kept looking at him, her lips crinkling—though he knew *she* wasn't about to cry—and he knew that she knew. That they'd somehow created this problem. This *developmental issue.* In Boston she'd been dressing herself, in the upside-down Somerville house with the cubbyhole basement bedrooms and the thumb-sized kitchen, the box of a living room and the one bathroom. Nine hundred square feet for as much as they were now paying for fourteen hundred square feet. This had been a move up. But now Sophie was constipated and backward and he had to wonder if they should have stayed. Four people in nine hundred square feet. Other people did it.

"Warner?"

She was next to him, holding him, her arms wrapped around his chest. He hugged her. They never hugged—who had time? He kissed her lips, she kissed his—slow, sweet, salty, not tongue, just lips, not sexual, but sensual. So maybe sexual. Yes, sexual. Could he have another one? There it was. Incredible. To think that it was always there and they could have it. Okay, not always. Only moments of always. Here in their eighth year of marriage, their twelfth year of together, their fifth year of children, he knew the range and the levels— the rareness of sex, the instants of passion, the impulses of loathing. When the kids roared around you and you roared at each other and you wondered, What the fuck am I doing in this? I never wanted this. I wanted Europe, women, South America, a lot of different bars, endless opportunity, endless challenge, endless uncertainty. Endless not knowing. Not this up at six, breakfast at seven, schools at eight, work at nine, schools at five, dinner at six, bedtime at eight, wine at nine *crap*. Not this weekend laundering, bathroom dousing, car servicing, grocery shopping, bargain hunting, closet cleaning *shit*. Fuck you for getting me into this. Fuck me for letting you. Fuck—

"Well," she said. She gave a shy tug on his belt.

He looked at her giving, generous, unlined face. A face he had known for a dozen years and still found amazement in. He couldn't even tell what color her eyes were—green or hazel, who the fuck knew? So there was comfort in being together. So you didn't have to go crazy. So he was all over the map tonight. Why should this night be different than any other night. Because on this night—

"Yes," he said. "Yes, please. Let's do."

Despite everything they began hunting for a house. They could not go higher than 150 and they preferred something a good deal lower. Sometimes they had to take the children with them, to nether SouthPark, the Arboretum, inner Elizabeth, lower Dilworth, Plaza Midwood, the fringe of Cotswold. At each place Sophie would wander the halls, flush the toilets in the bathrooms, turn on and off lights. "Is this going to be our house?" she'd ask. "Is this? Is this?"

They danced with one agent and the next and the next,

not committing, always trying to get into the right place before anyone else could. It was a crazy market and anything wonderful went before it was even listed, always at the asking price or higher. A broker named Neal kept calling and leaving packets on their doorstep. The houses were all inevitably tiny or dingy or sterile boxes. Ten days into January Milicent called. "A place on the corner of Winthrop and Tremont," she said breathlessly into the answering machine. "Lower Dilworth—can you believe it? It's perfect for you all. You'll love it. The agent's name is Bobbie Ray Bingham. I don't know her or anything. It hasn't gone on the market yet. If you can get ahold of her today, you can get in there before anyone else. At the least you ought to drive by and see what you think. Let me know."

They drove by. It was a corner house with yellow vinyl siding, a big yard. Three bedrooms, a changing-for-the-better block of lower Dilworth. They left a message on Bobbie Ray's pager. In the evening she called.

"All right," she said. "Because it's you and you're a family and it being a new year and all, I can get you in there tomorrow at eight-thirty. Does that work?"

"Yes," Megan said.

"That's lucky. Because it goes on the market at ten and we've had a half-dozen serious calls already."

She showed at eight-thirty in a black Lexus.

"You're on time," she called out, popping from the car in a white cowboy hat, a pair of gold chains around her neck, white hair coiffed and blown back from the sides of her face. She handed them each her card with a color picture of her in the hat: Bobbie Ray Bingham, $2,000,000 Club. "And these are the children." She bent to Sophie and offered her hand.

"I'm Bobbie Ray Bingham, sweetheart, and you know what, I bet you anything you all are going to be living here."

She led them around back to a wide deck and a door with a lock box, opened it up, and stepped aside. "Take your time, take your time. You need to be sure. I'll just stand to the side and be available for any questions. You won't get a hard sell from me. This property doesn't need it."

Warner carried in Daniel, and Megan took Sophie's hand. Through a shotgun kitchen was an L-shaped living room that wrapped around what could be the nursery, sided on two walls by French doors. The master bedroom had a narrow, new white shower with a built-in ledge you could sit on while you bathed. Sophie's room fronted the street next to a large, wood-paneled dining room, off of which was a sunroom with a concrete floor and a fireplace. The pull-down attic steps ascended to a fully reinforced storage space that could be broken out with dormer windows and new flooring.

"This could work," Megan said.

The heat seemed strong, the air-conditioning faint. There was no basement. But it was all wood floors, white walls save for the dining room and master bedroom, a lot of generous windows.

"You have our checkbook?" he whispered to Megan.

"Yes," she said.

They went out and walked around the house. It was larger on the inside, pleasingly broken up, but the lot was big and there was a storage shed at the end of the gravel driveway.

"A block or two," Bobbie Ray delicately pointed out, "to stores and shops."

"Well," Warner said. He turned to Megan. "What do you think?"

"What do *you* think?"

They seemed to be smiling insanely at each other.

"What do we do now," Warner asked Bobbie Ray. "We've never bought a house before."

"First-time buyers?" Bobbie Ray threw out her arms in welcome. "I *love* it." Quickly she explained that if they really truly did like the house, if they really truly were ready to make an offer, then they should go back to her office and put in the bid. All they'd need was a check for the earnest.

"Well?" Warner said to Megan.

"Well?" Megan said.

"I guess we'll follow you," he told Bobbie Ray.

At the carpeted, ringing office Bobbie Ray dished up lollipops for the kids and pens and forms for the parents. The asking price was $141,000, but if you wanted to be sure, if you really wanted to be sure, you needed to make your best offer first, Bobbie Ray said.

"Does it have to be higher?" Megan asked.

"Doesn't have to be. Now, I'm your agent. I'm not the seller's agent, and my job is to advise you. Of course it doesn't have to be. But it could be, and it should be if you're really sure, if you really want it accepted."

"How would that work," Warner said flatly. "I mean, how much more are we talking here?"

"Not a lot. Could be a thousand more, could be two, could be five hundred. Depending on how strongly you all felt."

"I think," Megan said, looking directly at Warner, "that we feel pretty strongly."

"I do," Warner said. "I do. I just don't know that we need to offer *more*."

"You don't," Bobbie Ray said. "You don't. You offer what you're comfortable with. You offer what's in your heart."

"Yes," Warner said.

Behind them on the floor the children began to swirl.

"It's almost ten," Bobbie Ray said. "Do you all need a minute by yourselves?"

"Please," Warner said, scooping up Daniel.

Bobbie Ray stepped from behind her desk and smiled warmly at them. "I love you all like I love my own children," she said. "I wouldn't want you all to do whatever wasn't absolutely best for you."

Warner smiled stonily and Megan just looked at her. Bobbie Ray shut the door behind her.

"Creepy," he said.

"They're all creepy," Megan said.

"I want another lollipop," Sophie said.

"A thousand or five hundred isn't that much," Megan tried.

"A thousand or five hundred is a thousand or five hundred," Warner said.

"So what are you saying?" Her face reddened. "That you want to offer only the price? I thought you liked the house."

"I do, I do."

"If we don't buy this house, we're not buying a house," Megan said.

"We're not buying a house?" Sophie began to shriek.

"Honey," Warner said. Something in his tone was terrible, and Daniel exploded in tears. Warner held him. Someone knocked on the door and Bobbie Ray poked her head in, strode in holding her hands behind her back.

"Look what I have!" she said suddenly. She brought out a matching zebra cat Beanie Baby for each child. Instantly the children fell quiet. "You all can keep them," she said, handing them over. She sat back behind her desk. "So what did you all decide?" she said softly.

Megan and Warner looked at each other and said nothing.

"Why don't you," Bobbie Ray pushed the form toward Warner, "write the number you feel best about on the line that says bid."

"Okay," he said. He wrote $141,000 and showed it to Megan. She nodded without expression. He slid the form back to Bobbie Ray.

"That's fine," she said. "That's fine." She smiled at them. "Now what about the earnest? You can go as low as a thousand and as high as you want, though you really don't need to go higher than four or five thousand."

"A thousand," Warner said.

"A thousand's fine," Megan said. She pulled out the checkbook and wrote the check.

"Is that it?" Warner asked.

"That's it!" Bobbie Ray rose and shook both their hands. "We'll have the offer in to their listing agent in about ten minutes, and we'll know within seventy-two hours, I believe."

"Thank you," Warner and Megan said. They all shook hands again.

"Congratulations!" Bobbie Ray said.

In the car Megan said, "I suppose I'll never have a house."

"Oh we'll get a house," he said as he drove them back toward Crape Myrtle Hill. "I just don't think it *has* to be that house."

"You didn't like it?" she said. "Then why did we make an offer?"

"Oh, I liked it," he said. "It was a little dark, is all. A little small, a little tight. But I liked it."

"Whatever," she said.

The first day after the seventy-two hours Monique put through a call from Bobbie Ray Bingham. Warner picked up the phone, bracing himself.

"Is this Mr. Warner Lutz?" Bobbie Ray asked.

"Hey, Bobbie Ray," he said.

"I mean," she said, and he could hear the triumph pouring from her voice, "is this Mr. Warner Lutz, the *new homeowner*!"

"You're kidding me!" he said, his throat filling with an undeniable elation. "You're just kidding me."

"No, sir," she met his loudness. "No sir. You get your home at your price. You stuck to your guns and showed us all something."

"Unbelievable!" he roared back at her. "Unbelievable. This is wonderful news. I've got to call Megan. Thank you so much, Bobbie Ray."

"Thank you," she said, "thank you. You go ahead now and I'll be in touch later on in the day."

Instantly he dialed Megan. "Hey," he said, "we got it!"

"What?" She was truly startled. She'd already given up on it.

"The house," he said. "We fucking got the house."

"Oh, Warner!"

Between them they delegated the mortgage broker, the inspector, the task of collecting all the files for the financing. On the phone she seemed to kiss him good-bye. "I love you," she said.

He walked giddily out into the office, grinning. He felt

as if he'd just had another child, or won a kind of award. He felt as if he ought to be handing out cigars. He was a home-owner! It was a sweet little house, really perfect for them at this stage of their lives. And in three or five years, the way things went around here, the resale value would be astronom-ical. Well, maybe not astronomical, but pretty damn good. He thought of telling Fenton but Fenton had cancer and news of the future seemed inappropriate. He didn't really know Monique. The others were all out on projects. He wished he could tell someone. He was a homeowner! He strolled back to his office and sat down. What a sweet little house. What a sweet little neighborhood. Now they'd be really living in the South. Now it would all feel like an adventure to him. Lower Dilworth. Unbelievable.

"Richard, line two," Monique said over the intercom.

"Hello, there," Warner said.

"Hello yourself. I got a lead for you over at TransOne."

"Terrific!"

Richard fed him the name and number. "How much do we have in so far?"

"Fifteen," Warner counted. "But that ought to climb quickly."

"It'd better. What are we short now, two-sixty?"

"Uh-hunh. But fifteen in new corporate money for an organization that has never had corporate support before, in all of six weeks, that's not bad."

"I guess not," Richard admitted.

"Hey," Warner said, "I bought a house."

"What?" Richard said quickly.

"Megan and I, we had our offer on a house accepted."

"Well." Richard paused. "Well, well. Good for you! When's the closing?"

"Thirty days, I think."

"Good. Good, good. Listen, I've got to run. I'll talk to you soon. Call TransOne, all right?"

"Right," Warner said. He hung up and looked at the phone. So Richard wasn't that happy about the house. But Warner *was* turning things around. They did have new money coming in. Not a lot, but some, and it had come quickly. Fifteen was fifteen, was what he knew. It was a hell of a lot better than nothing.

Mid-January. The smallest icicles forming on trees before the wind shakes them off, the cold wet patina of the weather over the asphalt and clay, mottling the car windows. Bald days of sunshine on dulled strip malls set free from their Christmas encasements. Only the relief of Martin Luther King Day. On a hunch, Megan was going to keep the gallery open. Warner dropped her off and took the two children with him to his shut office.

Anyone who worked knew this was the only time to work—when no one else was in, when the phone didn't ring, when there was no one to fax or e-mail. He set Daniel down on the floor with an activity blanket and gave Sophie a few wads of Post-its, three pens, and a dozen binder clips. He figured he had fifteen minutes before the first eruption.

He was several lines into finally settling on a mortgage package when the phone rang. He could let the machine pick up, but it was probably her. Maybe she had changed her mind and would call off the second half of her day.

"Hey," he answered.

"Is that you, Warner?" It was Richard. "I figured I might find you in."

"I'm here," he said.

"Listen, there's something I need to get with you about. You going to be around for a few minutes?"

"A few minutes? I think so."

"I'll be right over." He hung up before Warner could tell him about the kids.

Warner looked at them. He didn't have much else to occupy them, but Richard had said it would take only a few minutes. He cleared his desk of the mortgage stuff and broke out more pens and Post-its to toss to the children in case they didn't last. For the moment Sophie was drawing a picture onto each frame of a bound wad of Post-its. He heard Richard let himself in with his key, then he was at the door. He stood there cautiously, frowning slightly at the kids. "Do you have a moment?" he said.

"Of course. Sorry about the children."

Richard took a chair and pulled it up beside him. Warner reached to flick on the computer.

"No need for that," Richard said.

Warner leaned back. "So what's up?" he said, stowing whatever dread he felt.

"The board has been talking." Richard folded his hands on his lap. "We *are* pleased about the progress you've been able to make since the Due South debacle; don't get us wrong. But we think"—he coughed and looked discreetly at the children, lowered his voice to a hush—"we think it might not quite be the right time for you to buy a house in Charlotte."

"What the—" He stopped himself. "Hey, Sophie sweetie?"

She looked up stone-faced from her project.

"Why don't you get yourself a cup of water from the cooler out front. Okay?"

"Okay, Daddy." She got up smiling and stepped from his office.

"So what's this all about?" he asked Richard.

"It's a simple thing, really," Richard said. "You're still on probation. You know that. When we heard you were closing on a house we just wanted you to be aware of the fact that we still haven't decided yet on extending the one-year contract, of which currently there are less than eight months left. We felt we had an obligation to let you know that."

"I am aware of the situation," Warner heard himself say, "but there is new money coming in and I do anticipate a full recovery."

"So do we. So do we." Richard smiled. "We just don't know that this is the right time for you to buy a house in Charlotte, and I've now told you that." He rose from his chair. "So everything is out in the open. As it should be. Thanks for taking the time to see me."

"Thank you," Warner said.

"Nice to see you again, Sophie," Richard called on his way out.

"Bye," she called after him. "Bye."

So they really didn't want him to buy a house. So they were more than not sure about him. Fuck them; he would get another job in Charlotte if it came to that. No he wouldn't. It would have to be elsewhere. But it wasn't over here yet, he could still turn it around. They could buy that fucking house if they wanted. Or they could try to back out. He'd known they shouldn't have bought it in the first place—it was too tight, too soon, too much for what it was, too fucking wrong.

"Daddy?" Sophie said quietly, spilling water on the floor. "Why doesn't Mr. Thrasher want us to buy a house?"

"Oh," he said, blushing in front of his four-year-old. "Oh, that's not what he said at all. He said that maybe the winter was the wrong time to buy and that we could do better in the spring."

"Oh," she said seriously.

Daniel gave an angry shout as he tried to tug his blanket out from under himself. Warner ought to get them out of here. Why had they bought that house? How much would it cost to get them out of it? His head felt like it had been cracked down the middle. He had to think his story through before he could tell Megan. She might want to try to buy the house anyway and there he'd be seven months into a thirty-year mortgage and without a job and then what? She always got to make the decisions. Fucking Megan. Fucking house. Fucking kids. Fucking Charlotte. Fucking him.

Through the wall of his headache he packed up the kids and drove along Uptown looking for distractions. Buses fronted the entrance of Discovery Place and through the windows he could see several hundred kids crowding the vending machines. In the backseat Daniel began to cry as the noon glare spilled over his sun shade. Warner headed south for the suburbs. Sophie kicked his seat back so hard he swore his kidneys shuddered.

"I *wanted* to go to Discovery Place!"

He drove for twenty minutes while alternately she shrieked at him and Daniel bawled and he patiently—or so he thought—explained that they were going to that great playground they'd been to months before that not too many people seemed to know about and they could have free rein. It took him overlong to define "free rein," and he was sorry he had mentioned it. In the cloistered parking lot were two gleaming minivans, both with their rear doors flung open to the rising heat and the astonishing emptiness. His headache eased.

"This is great!" Sophie said as he unbuckled her and let her climb from the booster. He reached for Daniel and watched her skip across the lot into the safety of the swings.

The playground was on a ridge above overturned fields of clay that were awaiting development. Two bejeweled and made-up mothers swung their toddlers in the infant swings as they talked, casting an obvious eye on Warner, who felt underdressed and as far as he could tell the only white guy not working today. Daniel kept trying to broach the distance through a pebbled pool and a spray of green, and Warner kept tugging him back. He screamed. There was a third infant swing but he'd have to stand over there with the mothers. He thought they were talking about restaurants. Again Daniel got away and he thought, why shouldn't he be able to swing with the minivan set? He picked up the boy, carried him over, nodded at the mothers not three feet away, and set him in the seat. Gently he pushed him. Daniel gave a squeal, and he pushed harder. He moved to the front of the swing so he didn't have to stand directly next to the women. In between pushes he tugged his baseball cap low. He wanted to be as unseen as possible, anonymous. They probably thought he was unemployed.

They wore charm bracelets and oversize earrings and pastel sweaters. Their hair was poofed, sculpted, and neatly laced with blonde. Pencil-thin eyebrows arched above their sunglasses. Their children were named Tyler and Tiffany.

"He said I could have a house for five hundred or six hundred," Tyler's mother was saying, "or I could have a house for less and get a second home at the beach."

Daniel cooed at Tyler.

"Push harder, Mommy," he said. "That baby's catching up."

"Well," Tiffany's mother said, "Kevin told me that in two years I could have any house I wanted, regardless of the price."

"Did you see Rhonda's floor plan?"

Tiffany's mother harrumphed. "All *she* wants is a big-ass house so she can throw her big-ass parties."

"Are you happy, sweetie," Warner murmured to his son. "A few more pushes and we'll try the slide."

"That outfit she wore to Calvary last week." They both laughed.

"What do you expect from somebody who tassels her candlesticks?"

"She did do that amazing auction for Big Brothers."

"She did." Tiffany's mother sighed and pushed the slipping sunglasses up her nose. "This house thing is driving me crazy. I told Kevin so what if we can afford eight thousand a month on rent. It doesn't mean we want to pay it."

"Daddy!" Sophie yelled from her swing.

"You're thinking of *renting*?" Tyler's mother said.

"I am *not* buying just any house, and new construction is so feeble around here. I want a home with some character."

"Like the one you've got."

"That's right, darling. Just twice as big." On the backswing she tousled Tiffany's head. "We will have at least another little one. Maybe two or three. I'm thinking six thousand square feet."

Tyler's mother nodded soberly. "That makes sense."

"Of course we'll redo whatever we buy. I just don't want to buy new."

"Daddy!" Sophie called again.

"Okay, buddy." His voice was a whisper as he levered Daniel from the swing. Furiously the baby kicked at him. Under the baseball cap his head was in full sweat. He hurried over to Sophie. "What's up?"

"I want to go on the baby swing," she said.

"Honey." In his arms the baby screamed. He would not look back. "You're too old for the baby swing."

"I *want* to."

"I'll push you."

"No." She graveled to a stop and plunked off the swing. "I'm going."

He caught her shoulder. Why couldn't anything be easy? Why couldn't he let her go? "I said no."

"I can climb in myself." She ran toward the swing. Daniel wriggled and he let him down. Instantly he began to crawl after her. Warner scooped him up and held him like a barrel under his arm. Sophie was climbing into the swing.

"You want a push, honey?" Tyler's mother asked her. "Is that all right?" she called to Warner.

He nodded yes, his throat too thick to talk. She pushed both children, her bracelets jangling. Her painted fingernails glittered in the sun. "You're a good pumper," she said.

"I'm four," Sophie said.

"This is Tyler. He's nearly two. Can you say hello, Tyler?"

"Push me higher, Mommy!" Tyler said.

"That's my brother Daniel. He's almost one."

"What a big sister you are!" She gave Warner a little smile. "She's adorable."

"Thank you," Warner said. She kept pushing Sophie and he stood by awkwardly, holding the squirming Daniel, trying to figure out a sociable way to extricate the girl. He felt guilty for interrupting the day of these two women and their children and their stocked minivans and their plans for big-ass houses. It was one-thirty. "Shall we go see Mommy?" he said, immediately sorry he'd suggested it.

"Mommy?" Sophie said, trying to climb from the seat in midswing.

"Nama," Daniel gave out. "Nama!"

"I guess they really want to go visit their mommy!" Tyler's mother grinned as she lifted Sophie from the swing and set her down in front of Warner.

"I guess so," Warner said. "Thanks again. You all have a nice day."

Sophie gave her his hand and he walked the now docile children to the car and buckled them in their seats. What was another twenty-minute car trip when they were happy and manageable? They drove north, back toward the office and the gallery, back toward Uptown, passing backhoes and piles of orange clay and nearly hidden coves of tightly packed subdivisions and walled enclaves of newly built monstrous houses and then through relatively old Myers Park where the houses were redbrick and the air reeked of plantation money that had fled Charleston at the end of the Civil War and for the briefest of instants you had a scent of history. Here, at $250 a square foot, was a place he'd never be, with garishly thick-trunked trees and plucked lawns out his car window on such a fine January day with the children content in the backseat and the car gliding through the momentary synchronicity of the stoplights. They slid by the hospitals and passed an old stone and gabled church islanded by wide new roads, then climbed the faint rise to Uptown.

It was two o'clock when he carried one child and pulled the other through the gonging door of the gallery.

"It's us," he called, trying to still the tremor of his voice as he loosed the kids on the carpet.

She came out holding a hammer, with a nail still clenched between her teeth. She tried to smile. "This isn't a good time," she said, taking the nail from her mouth. "Milicent's chosen today to have me start crating up our best pieces, and the phone's been ringing off the hook."

The children swarmed to her and she picked them up one at a time, still holding on to the hammer and nails, and kissed them briskly and set them down.

"I thought this was gravy," he said. "You aren't even supposed to be open. You're not moving till April, for Christ's sake." He snatched Daniel out of reach of a pedestaled piece of limestone. He picked him up, and the baby yowled.

"She's got this idea that we can place our best pieces in the lobby. The foot traffic is incredible, she says. They've got a cappuccino stand and seven thousand bankers and lawyers passing by every few hours. Where'd Sophie go?"

He looked underfoot and around the room and glanced into the first interior space. "Sophie?" he called. "Well, she is four and a half," he muttered.

"It's just . . ." She threw up her hands and headed back toward the inventory. "There's all this really expensive stuff around. You know that."

"I know, I know." He wrestled with Daniel as he hurried back. Sophie wasn't in any of the four showrooms. She wasn't in the back office or in the corridor stocked with glass art.

"Sophie!" they called. "Sophie!"

"Wait," he said. He strode with Daniel bent over his

shoulder to the bathroom and flung open the door. There she sat, her face red from pushing, her hands clasped into a knot.

"Read to me," she said.

He shook his head and shut the door.

"Warner!" Megan said. "Don't slam the door in her face."

"I didn't slam it. I shut it."

"You slammed it. I was standing right here."

He set Daniel down and immediately the baby started off toward an open pack of nails. "Goddamn it." He gathered him up again. "This place is a fucking wreck."

"Do you want me to take the kids?" she said, her voice eerily calm. "Is that it? Give me him."

"No, no," he said. He backed away.

"You can't stand it when I'm working and you're not, is that it?" she said.

"Is that it, is that it," he said, trying to keep his ground and still hold the baby from her.

"You are such a fucking baby," she said.

"Sophie," he said through the door. "Come on, honey. Mommy has to work. We're going to Latta Plantation instead."

From inside she gave a squeal of delight.

"Martyr," Megan said.

He set Daniel down again and yanked the hammer from her hand. "Give me the nails," he said. "You deal with him until she gets out."

She looked at him and shook her head. But she gave him the nails and took up Daniel.

"Now where's that fucking crate," he said. "This ought to be cathartic."

"Honey." She touched his wrist. "You can hammer all you want. But not that crate. You don't have the training."

He followed her eyes and saw the damn crate. "I can bang a fucking nail," he said.

"I'm telling you—"

"Just shut up. I'm going to take the kids and get out of here, but I'm going to finish your damn crate first."

"What the hell has gotten into you?" She tried to follow him back but the baby clawed at her face.

"Nothing," he said. "Some mothers at the playground, that's all." He strode back to the crate. It was half nailed shut. "I don't see why you can't carry them the four blocks," he said.

"That's not the way we do things," she said. "I really wish—"

He shot her a look. The look he had when she didn't recognize him at all. When you couldn't say anything to him. She had those moments, too. Once when Sophie was three months old Warner had said something to Megan that she couldn't even now remember, and then kept talking when she asked him to be quiet, and she'd gone and slammed their brand-new $250 stroller around the apartment until one of the wheels broke off and the canopy had bent double. And the time he'd goaded her too far and she'd smashed their $121 remote control into the floor so many times that it finally split and its insides spilled out. Now she walked the baby into another room and shut her eyes as she swayed him, feeling how sleepy he was, how soon he'd nap and there'd be peace. In a moment she heard the diligent pounding of the hammer. Sophie hummed from behind the bathroom door. The hammer tapped. There was a slight tinkle, like a chime.

"Oh," he said softly.

"What," she said, hurrying back with the baby. Though she knew what it was.

He was prying open the nailed crate, his neck and face brightly flushed.

"Why do you even sell this glass shit," he said quietly.

"Because it's *art,* Warner. That's why." She pulled him out of the way and peered inside, the baby against her ear. A fracture ran through the heart of the sculpture. If she lifted it, it would break in two and then into countless tiny pieces. "It's nothing," she said bitterly. "A couple of thousand dollars." She turned and looked at him and handed him the baby. "Now would you please get the hell out of here so I can do my job."

"I'm sorry," he said. He gave her back the hammer.

"Sometimes you just can't stop yourself, can you?"

"You—"

"And you can't even take it without dishing it out."

"Whatever," he said. "Sophie!"

She opened the bathroom door and smiled at them. "All done," she said.

He held out his hand to her and she took it and he walked her and carried Daniel to the door. "Later," he said, without looking back, the damn gong gonging as he hurried them through.

"Have a good time," she said.

He marched the kids to the Honda, stuck them in their seats, backed out of the space, and pulled from the lot. Daniel was whimpering in a near catatonic state preparatory to a nap, and Sophie was humming a song she was struggling to make up. He should have just left them there. Goddamn him for trying to pack glass art. Goddamn her for being so goddamn sanctimonious. He'd never wanted to be a father, and she'd never comprehended how it would be to have the holy triad of children, career, and him. He angrily kicked at the brake for the first of many stoplights out of town just to get to the goddamn interstate where he'd have to drive twenty goddamn miles to the exit and another fifteen minutes to the plantation and by the time he got there he'd be exhausted and the kids would be rested and he'd scramble after them along the lake and down the dock and then Sophie would insist on going to see the raptors and he'd pay the fucking donation at the door and they'd wait around for the next guided tour and then he'd stand there juggling Daniel while the guards prattled on about birds of prey for forty or fifty minutes and it would be nearly dark before they got out of there and were back in their goddamn crowded car for the forty-five-minute trip back to pick up Megan and the kids could conceivably fall asleep on the way and there they'd all be at home in the dark with a full day of work ahead tomorrow and the kids fighting their bedtimes because they were overnapped and whose goddamn fault was that? Volunteering Latta Plantation didn't make him a martyr; it made him goddamn stupid. Like messing with that goddamn glass. Like the way he'd handled Richard today.

At the third consecutive stoplight that he managed to hit he noticed the incredible silence. The sweet silence. They were asleep. He pulled over to a loading zone. If he didn't drive them up to Latta they wouldn't nap twice, but what could he do with them that would appease them? Goddamn her for working. *He* wasn't working. She was so goddamn self-righteous. He didn't have *the training*. What the fuck did that mean? Did they teach you how to crate art in grad school? He couldn't have imagined a more useless degree. He knew he was loathsome now, just vituperative, just dumb, but god how he hated her sometimes. Hated how particular she was about the town house and the chores and the regimented weekends and the work schedule. Hated how she insisted on making everything equal. Wasn't he the one who made more money? Hadn't he been the one who'd been against having kids in the first place? She should be doing it all. He glanced in the backseat. When they slept they were so innocent and appealing. Sometimes he could just—

A fist rapped at his window. Warner rolled it down in front of the brown uniform of a UPS guy. He abruptly nodded at the children in the backseat.

"Excuse me, sir," he said quietly. "I've been politely flashing my lights at you for the past five minutes. *This* is a loading zone. Could you get the fuck out of here?"

His face was obliteratingly hot as he started the car. Now what? He could park someplace and wait out their naps, but if he drove around they'd nap more deeply. If he drove them the twenty minutes home and unloaded them they'd wake on the transfer and be undernapped. If only he could take them back to the gallery and lay them out on the floor on a bunch of blankets. The gong would probably wake them or she'd scream at him as he carried them in. God his head felt hot. He'd been up from four to six with Daniel and then he hadn't been able to fall back asleep. "You need to get used to that," she'd said, as if he'd manufactured his own sleep problems. His head screamed. One day he'd let her know the truth. Oh she knew it. He'd fought against having the first baby, yet once they'd agreed to have Sophie, and had actually *planned* it in agreement, he'd been good about her. But he'd been a total dick about the second pregnancy and for seven of its months he hadn't even helped her in any way especially and hadn't asked any questions. He'd made her feel alone. He'd tried to exact some kind of revenge. When the baby came, he had shut up and shared. But they both knew he'd been a dick. Now he loved Daniel. He truly did.

Never mind how it had torn them apart. Never mind how Megan had had her friends in from Chicago on the week of Sophie's birthday party, people they'd lived near in San Francisco back before everyone had to move to the next better job. Malcolm was a shrink and Claire was an *actor,* and at night when each of their children was asleep in Sophie's room downstairs, they'd bandied about the second-kid idea. "It's just so selfish not to," Claire had said. Malcolm nodded. "It's definitely unfair to the first child not to have the second child," he'd pedantically concluded. "It's the most natural thing in the world. The better question is how could you not?" Megan had sat there pressing her lips together. "That's ridiculous," Warner had argued. "Having the second kid isn't about the first kid and being *fair* and being *natural.* It's about your marriage and your life and how much each extra kid drains from that." "*Drains,*" said Claire. "*Drains.* That's the most ungenerous verb I've ever heard of." "All right, then *demands.*" "Better," Malcolm shook his head, "but not yet best. Have the second kid, Warner. We are." One evening Claire and Malcolm had been so intent on eating the pasta that they had all cooked together that they fought over who would watch their baby, who was only one and unusually cranky that night. They kept handing him back and forth while they ate. At three in the morning the baby woke everybody, and only then did the two of them figure out that they'd been so obsessed with their own dinners that they'd forgotten to feed him his. During the humid cleanup of Sophie's birthday party Claire commandeered the video camera while Warner muttered as he plucked confetti from the floor, "We are not having a fucking second kid."

Later, of course, he'd had to erase that part of the videotape, but he could never erase how Megan had set him up for the week, a week in which he'd felt badgered and ridiculed and selfish. One night after a particularly brutal argument in front of Malcolm and Claire he'd woken at two or three to find Megan's side of the bed empty. He climbed the stairs to the living room, peered around the steps not wanting to be seen, unsure if he could see two or three of them on the sofa or what the hell was going on, but he knew better than to get caught spying on her and her friends. He tiptoed back down to their room, waited, heard what he thought were voices and body rustle, fell asleep. Woke again a little later and still she wasn't there. When he woke at five, she was finally again in bed. She'd been gone so long he was astonished and grateful that she'd returned. They made love without contraception and then again a second time in the afternoon, before he definitely decided against the second child. Now they had two children. Now he might not even have a job. Now they had one car and no free weekends and everything they had saved was going toward buying a house that wouldn't be big enough and to socking Daniel into daycare at that wretched Baptist church. He loved Daniel and he loved Sophie; he wasn't about to belt them into the backseat and drive them into the lake. But Megan. He shook his head. Megan who had gotten her way about both kids and—it seemed to him—the house, too, decisions so life-changing that there were no decisions left to make. Megan he felt differently about. One day he'd let her know. One day he'd tell her. He shook his head at the umpteenth stoplight and wheeled around against it in a perfectly illegal U-turn. Fuck that. He wasn't fucking driving all the way to Latta Plantation and back.

She'd called the artist and he would wait to see what the insurance would do. She'd called the haulers and they were willing to delay until four-thirty. She had three more pieces to crate, then the pedestals to label and pack and then she was done. Milicent said they had to be installed before Tuesday at eight, when the bankers and lawyers would come streaming back from their minivacations. It would make a statement, she'd said. They would seem so fresh and sharp; it would be like some new beginning. She'd come by in the morning and they'd chosen the most striking and the most richly textured pieces they had. She knew how it was a good idea, but boy was she sick of Milicent.

The next piece was smaller, and she sat on the floor with it. She fitted it easily into its thin protective sheathing and then into the wood encasement. She got five or six nails and held some of them in one hand and stuck a few point-out in her mouth. She positioned the crate obliquely against the floor so if the art shifted or the crate slipped it would strike indirectly. That had been Warner's first error. She held the wooden lid firmly against the box and tapped one inch from the corner. Warner's second mistake—he aimed too close to the corner, putting too much pressure on the fineness of the fit. They'd be on the interstate by now, the winter light against Sophie's sunshade. They'd both be napping. When he parked and woke them, they'd be sweet with the fresh lake air and the thick scent of the pine trees and all that space to run around in, the long hill sloping close to the water, the challenge of the dock. He'd have to watch them on the dock. Briefly she worried, but he hadn't lost a kid yet. She knew he loved them. He'd fought them, all right, but he loved them.

The first corner was secure and she rotated the crate ninety degrees and began the second fit, again at least one inch in from the angle. Sometimes he hated her, she knew. These were phases he went through—oppressed by his work or the children or both—but it was still hate, real hate. She had told him he could leave. He wouldn't. She had told him he ought to have an affair. She couldn't tell if he had or not. She felt relatively certain that he hadn't. But she couldn't bear the hate. She never hated him. Or, she had, but only when his own loathing for her had pushed her and pushed her and she'd swung back, like she'd done today. Pure defense. A child's game: you hated me first, so I'll hate you back. He *was* a baby. They were all babies, all arms and legs flailing through the endless struggle of the day, the week, the year. She loved his active engagement in the struggle, that he was so conscious of it and railed against it while for so long she'd gone around internalizing everything. Yes, he was a whiner, but she'd seen him get beyond it. Together, it seemed to her, they'd got beyond a lot. Less so here than in other places.

Out front the gallery door gonged. The haulers. She took the nails out of her mouth.

"I'm back here," she called over her shoulder. She finished the second corner and rested the hammer above and behind her on the worktable. She double-checked the fit of the second corner. It was tight. In a way, she'd rather crate than sell. She could barely hear Ed behind her. But he was there.

"You can start with those." She nodded backward with her head. She rotated the small work to the third corner and reached behind her for the hammer.

In the briefest of instants, before it struck, before her brain filled with a million shattered thoughts, she wondered at the stupidity of her own behavior. How she'd spent her adult life being aware of dark streets and hidden corners and looming vans parked in mysterious fashion in a hundred lots in Boston and San Francisco and Charlotte. How she had an instinct for avoiding the dangerous, and that she knew she had a special reserve if it did set upon her. How in all that time she'd never been as exposed as she was now, her head tilted slightly back, tipping itself in a wretched offer, as it waited for the descent of the hammer.

When the call was put through by her secretary and she heard the tone of her son-in-law's voice as he said, "Nan"—the transportive thinness of it, as if it would connect her from this innocent moment of work to a place of immediate despair— she took her feet off the desk and set them on the floor, as a stillness rose from her stomach through her face. She felt hot all over. Her hands went cold. Her only girl. Her only two grandchildren. In the twelve years they'd known each other, he'd called perhaps twice: once to discuss Christmas presents, another time when he was arranging a surprise party for Megan. There had always been something off about him— how he never looked her in the eyes, the odd tales of his troubles at the various schools he'd gone to, just his general negativism. An edginess between them that could have been her natural distrust of men but was probably his misanthropy.

"Warner," she managed. "What is it?"

"She's in the hospital." He was crying. "She's not good. There was a break-in at the gallery. She was hit in the head.

Maybe more than once. She's unconscious. They aren't saying much."

"I'm on the next plane down." She was about to hang up. "Wait a minute. What hospital?"

"Memorial. ICU."

She hung up, intercommed Sandy, asked for the next flight out. It wasn't even five o'clock. A break-in at the gallery in the middle of the day? For what, credit card slips? Blown glass? Sandy intercommed that she had a car waiting, that a flight left in fifty minutes out of Hartsfield. That was Sandy. Nan picked up her mobile phone and purse.

"I'll call you," she told Sandy on her way to the elevator.

In the car she dialed the gallery. That was where they'd be.

A genteel voice insisted that the line was available only for official police business.

"I'm her mother," she said. Within a minute she was talking with a detective. The car was still stuck on Peachtree. She explained her impressions of Warner. God, this was how it happened. "No way," she concluded for the detective, "does he spend tonight with those children."

"I'm sorry, but we can't quite do that."

"For crying out loud," she said. "Have you talked with him?"

"You bet. We've talked with a lot of folks. We do hope to make an arrest shortly, but I can't say it will be tonight."

"Once," she said. "Once he hit her. It was ten years ago, but he did hit her."

"We're aware there is some history, ma'am."

"What?"

"We've spoken with the husband, ma'am. Is there anything else you'd care to tell us about the situation?"

"He hasn't incriminated himself yet, has he?"

"Ma'am." She could hear him flip paper. "The specifics of the case are continuing to evolve. Are there other folks you can suggest we contact to help us resolve this in the next few days?"

"Oh, god. The people he worked with. The people he went to school with. His parents even; they're honest people."

"We'll look into it."

"But *tonight*," she said.

"What time did you say you'd be down here?"

"Three hours."

"All right, then. I'm sure that we can certainly say that because we don't know what's happened here, the whole family warrants some protection. We'll see what we can do."

"That would be satisfactory. I'll speak to you soon."

She got a new dial tone and called the hospital. In a few long blocks they'd be on the highway. She would make her plane. A nurse came to the phone and confirmed that she was Megan's mother. "She has suffered severe head trauma," she said. "She's still in surgery."

"What's the prognosis?"

"There is none yet, Mrs. Kendall."

Nan shivered. She hated it when anyone called her that. She'd returned to her maiden name as soon as she'd separated from Megan's father. "Wait and see?" she asked.

"Wait and see," the nurse affirmed. "As I said, they're still in surgery, and perhaps we'll have some more information soon."

"Thank you." She snapped the phone shut. When she tried to breathe she found she was sobbing. Her only girl. She'd been the sweetest little baby, not a word of complaint. She'd started reading at four. By the time she was twelve and

Nan had moved them from her father's home, she was cooking them both dinner while Nan herself studied late at the library. Those years when she'd been in business school and Megan so seriously tended their apartment, Nan knew it hadn't been fair. Sometimes even now she sent her money or expensive gifts and Megan would wonder why and ask her to stop. Why? Because she was guilty. Because she had taken more than she'd given. Poor little girl. Megan would hate her for thinking that. She was tough—not as tough as Nan, but pretty resilient. She'd get through this. They'd all get through this. She flicked open the phone and called her florist.

He was asleep. Warner wasn't quite sure how he'd done it, but the baby was asleep. Outside the front door stood a cop. On the sofa before the blank television Sophie whimpered. She hadn't eaten, she hadn't gone to the bathroom. At times she screamed, howled, "I want my mommy, I want my mommy, I want my mommy." She was hyperventilating. She had hiccups. She had cried herself out but kept trying anyway. He checked the spy hole again, then once more gathered her up on the sofa, felt her trembling against him. He felt he should keep the phone to his ear, as if he could continuously listen to the nurse: now she's breathing through the tube; now they're changing IVs; now they're conferring on the CAT scan; now they're readying her for the MRI. He just wanted to be there. Sophie shook in his arms. His parents were driving through the night and wouldn't arrive until the morning. When Nan came she might be unpleasant. There was no one he could call. He just wanted to be at the hospital. Daniel coughed faintly. He just wanted to be with the children. This was how it happened, this was how their lives unraveled, this was how you realized you didn't have it so bad in the first place. He held Sophie.

"When is," she hiccuped, her eyes red-rimmed, "when is. When is Mommy coming?"

"I don't know, sweetheart." He held her gently, but he wanted to hold her tight. "Mommy's hurt. We have to wait."

"Are you. Are you. Are you going to call?"

"I just did, honey. They said we have to wait."

"I-want-to-see-her," she forced out. "Now."

"We can't," he said, as delicately as he could, even though it was the fifth time he'd had to say it.

"What did." Her belly beat against his arm. "What did the doctor say?"

"The doctor said he didn't know yet." It was better for both of them if she didn't talk.

"I-want-my-mommy-now."

"I know." He kissed her neck, flinched at the salt of her dried tears, rocked her carefully in his arms. "Grandma and Pop-Pop and Granny Nan are coming," he said.

"Why aren't Grandpa and Julie?"

"I left a message. They haven't called back yet." He glanced at his watch. It had been only ten minutes since he'd last spoken to the nurse. He wanted to call again. He should call every ten minutes. He should call every hour. He just wanted to know how she was doing at every moment. He felt beside him for the phone. It was there against his thigh.

"I have to go to the bathroom."

"Okay," he said. He started to rise from the sofa, to carry her. The warmth gushed over him. He was soaked. She was soaked. The sofa was soaked. She screamed. "It's okay," he said, "it's okay. It's okay." The door pounded. He carried her dripping to the door, the carpet spongy underfoot.

"Everything all right in here?"

"Absolutely," he said, the door open wide, cold coming in. She was shivering and silent. "Just an accident."

The broad face looked them up and down. "All right," he said, and reached in and pulled the door shut. Warner carried her upstairs and ran the bath. He couldn't tell whether she was shivering or hyperventilating. He pulled his shirt-sleeve to the elbow and tested the water. He dipped her in, shucking only the shoes.

"Daddy," she laughed weakly. "My clothes."

He pried the clothes from her a piece at a time and threw them at the sink. From the near cabinet he dug out toys and dropped them in. The lap of his pants and the legs were soaked. The waist of his shirt was wet. She'd drenched him. He wished he had trainers for her. What would Megan do? At least the bed had a special sheet. His own clothes were in the closet in Daniel's room, and he'd never got anything out of there after the baby had been put to bed. It all felt like too much to think about. He didn't want to think.

"Daddy?" Her arms were outstretched. "I'm ready to get out."

He helped her out and wrapped her with towels and helped her dry and helped get her into pajamas. She was tender and fresh from the bath. What now?

"Could you eat something?"

She nodded.

He carried her downstairs and sat her on the dry cushion of the sofa. She shook her head.

"I want to be with you."

It occurred to him that she'd stopped hyperventilating. He carried her to the kitchen and sat her on the chair.

"Mac and cheese?"

"Yes, please."

"Peas?"

"Okay."

He poured and boiled and microwaved while she watched. He took it all out to the table with a place mat and fork and cup of milk. He carried her to her seat. He was still sopping. She picked up her fork and looked at him.

"Daddy," she said. "Could you call?"

It was an hour. Thank god he could call. As he expected the nurse sounded a bit stiff with him. Megan was stable. Critical but stable. He hadn't been to the hospital. He couldn't imagine what she looked like. "Stable," he told Sophie. "That's good."

"Good." Sophie nodded her head up and down. "Can I talk to her?"

"Not yet."

From under his pillow on their bed he pulled out his pajamas and put them on.

"Are you going to bed, too?" Sophie asked. She had finished her dinner and briefly he felt glad, ticking off food, bath, potty. He said he could see himself going to bed pretty soon. He carried her piggyback upstairs and brushed her teeth for her. They sat on the bed and he read from *Little House on the Prairie.* He was determined to read until she told him to stop. He read about the time Laura was only four or five or three, how her pa called her a little half-pint of cider half drunk up and how her dog got washed away fording a river and reappeared miles and days later at their campfire on the Nebraska plain. After forty minutes she said she'd heard enough. He'd never read to her that long before. His throat was empty. He kissed her good night.

Downstairs he eyed the wine in the refrigerator. He

should eat something. He forced down a banana and drank a glass of water as he stood at the kitchen sink. He tiptoed up to check on Sophie; she was asleep.

In the living room he sat on the sofa beside the wet part, with the phone on his lap, staring at the bed, and waited for Nan. He thought she might go to the hospital first and then come so he could go in.

Then, there was the issue of clothes. He stuck his damp sticky stuff in the washer and looked around for anything else to add. There were the sheets—Nan might sleep here, and he might sleep at the hospital. He dumped in the sheets. He turned on the water and shut the closet doors against the noise. He ran water and soap into a dish towel and blotted at the sofa and the carpet. The stains grew darker and darker. He took the cushions off. Coins and marbelized bits of food rolled onto the floor. The sofa seemed soaked to the springs. He peeled off the coverings of the cushions. The upholstery felt damp through. He couldn't just stick them in the dryer. He sat on the bed looking at the deconstructed sofa. There were faint crusted slicks of oatmeal and jelly from Daniel and Sophie. He and Megan had agreed the sofa was ratty and not worth cleaning or slipcovering. They were going to buy a new one in hunter green. They were going to have the carpet cleaner every three months, a housekeeping service every two weeks, a baby-sitter every Friday or Saturday night so they could go out on what she called dates. She liked the movies and he liked dinners in bright, crowded restaurants. They both liked dessert at bookstore cafés. In cities with sidewalks he liked window shopping and she liked going in. Unless it was a bar or a bookstore, he couldn't stand going in. They liked travel guides and he liked to look through books about wine and scotch, although he never bought them. He liked to know if what he liked was what people who knew liked. He wouldn't pay more than fifteen dollars for a bottle of wine, but for scotch he'd pay up to forty-five on his birthday or something. She'd bought him one for last Father's Day. Lagavulin. He was shocked. He'd thought she condemned his scotch drinking. But Lagavulin. A ninety-five rating. He nursed it for a month. Forty-two dollars. Sometimes it bothered him that Sophie knew about wine and scotch, although they most often waited until she was in bed. In front of her they talked about vino blanco seco: don't forget the vino blanco seco; could you pick up some vino blanco seco; is there any vino blanco seco in the fridge for later? They spelled sitter. They discussed escuela. They used to have pet names for each other but now they only had pet names for the children. Pookie. Cuddlebug. Moose. Lagavulin. He was crying. He'd almost cried when she'd given it to him. What kind of sickness was that?

He heard the light but frantic tapping at the front door only after it had been going on a bit. She must have been afraid of waking the children. His clothes were still in the wash cycle. She stood on the front stoop with the police officer.

"Hi, Nan," he said. In his flannel pajamas he felt like a child.

"Warner." She walked in without kissing him. That made sense. The police officer followed, uninvited. Warner felt less certain about that.

"How is she?"

She stood looking at the pieces of the sofa. "The same."

Behind him the police officer coughed awkwardly. "Sir?"

"They need you to go in for an interview," Nan said

quickly, as if she didn't have the patience for the officer's attempt at diplomacy.

"Now?" Warner said.

"Now," Nan said decisively.

"My clothes," he stammered. "My clothes are in the wash."

"You must have other clothes, Warner." She was speaking to him the way he felt in his pajamas.

"They're in Daniel's room. I'm not going to wake him. Look." He turned to the police officer. "Can't this wait another hour or two?"

"Sir." His hand moved toward him slightly, in the vaguest threat.

Warner wanted to look at Nan, but he couldn't. He tied on his sneakers and drew out his long coat from the hall closet. Not even a pair of sweats. He wanted to tell her about the children, what they liked for breakfast, their schedule. He couldn't even bear to look at her. He shrugged on his coat.

"Let's go," he said.

In the police car—would he ever forget this ride?—he sat in the back, locked in, and stared out at screen and mesh. It was a plain, bare, wide vinyl seat like some kind of couch or booth. He wasn't cold or hot. He wasn't anything. He kept his mouth shut. As they pulled down Crape Myrtle Drive he imagined he saw the fluttering of curtains opening and closing, the careful curiosity of his neighbors whose names sat snugly in his Rolodex for a job he was beginning to sense was no longer his. Out Providence they drove, the trees tall and slender, the dark ride in the hushed car interrupted only by an occasional crackle from the two-way radio. Was this an ending or a beginning? He felt himself wishing his life were over, that he lay safe in a casket, sealed off from everything, from the sweetness of the children, of her, the way she smelled as she gathered herself for work, soap scent, a waft of perfume, the soft water from the shower, tropical shampoo. How her kiss tasted after a sip of wine. Now they were passing the stores and shop fronts of Myers Park—Mars Park, they'd first thought it was called by the lush accents, Mars Park—gourmet coffee, gourmet Italian take-out, gourmet ice cream, gourmet bagels. The car rocked so gently it was like a boat, and they sailed along the border of Elizabeth, one of those up-and-coming neighborhoods that had been almost accessible to them, a place where they had looked. The shadows of overhead hospital skyways crossed within the car. Uptown blazed through the windshield. He shut his eyes against it.

"Does it bother you?" Ruth asked him for the second time. "Because if it does, I'll stop."

"It's all right." Alan's voice was graveled in depression. "It doesn't bother me."

Again she bent over her lap desk with the little penlight. "You could listen to the radio," she said. "It wouldn't bother me."

"I don't," he shook his head slowly, "want to listen to the radio."

"You think they have something about it?"

"Not in Virginia, they don't."

She looked out the window at nothing. "We got stuck around here once. You remember?"

"The lug nut on the right rear wheel of the trailer." He refused to perk up. "In Richmond. I remember."

"He was funny then. Everybody else, they wanted to eat

and sleep and watch television. He wanted to go see Poe's house."

"He was ten," Alan said flatly.

"Eight, I think. How he knew who Poe was, I still don't know."

Alan shrugged. "They were reading him in school."

"At eight? I don't think so. I took him and he went all around, read everything. Then he made me buy him a couple of sketches captioned by lines from 'The Raven.'"

Alan grunted. "He was always a dark kid."

"We can't condemn him." She'd said it quietly, matter-of-factly, so as not to attract attention to the unsayable.

"No." He paused. "But we might."

"You think they'll ask us questions?"

"Sure."

Now she could continue filing. They could talk about it. "Do we know anything?"

He tapped the steering wheel. "We know what we know. That's what we know."

She sighed and shrank within herself. Sometimes she could crest her despair, but mostly it deflated her, made her want to crawl into someplace and turn off any remaining light. Oh god he was guilty, and they'd raised him. She'd raised him. That temper that she'd never broken. The negativism, the bitterness. People were bitter. Alan was bitter. She was bitter. But Warner. She'd hit her kids, she'd smacked them if they talked back or behaved badly. It was what you did then; as far as she knew, for some people it was still what was done. But there had been a Saturday afternoon. He was eleven, sullen. They'd been arguing, screaming at each other. She could not recall it all. "Do you want to hit me?" she cried. "Go ahead, hit me." She offered him her face. He reared back and slapped it, hit her cheek so hard that her whole head turned, so that a redness stained her skin. He'd slapped her. That was what she knew. Tears seemed to start in her throat. "He hit me once," she said, her voice a rasp.

"What?" Alan said. His foot slipped on the gas and then recovered pressure.

"A long time ago, he slapped me in the face. I never told you. I asked him if he wanted to and he went ahead and smacked me."

"Oh." His voice sounded terrible, distant. "I wonder who else he's hit."

"Do we tell them?"

"If they ask." He was breathing heavily through his nose, the way he did when he was angry. He gave a snort. "They'll ask."

"He was only eleven. He was angry. I made him angry. I used to hit him. I used to hit all the kids."

"I was there."

"Maybe I didn't hit him enough."

"Maybe."

"Maybe I shouldn't have hit him at all."

"Four kids." Alan shrugged. "You had to hit them. It was the only way to manage."

"I can't remember all of it." She was crying. "It was a lot of work, you know. They'd just run around all day if I didn't line them up sometimes and punish them."

"I know."

"It was never gratuitous." What an odd word, she thought, as soon as she'd said it. "Maybe I mean arbitrary."

Alan sighed. "I understand you both ways."

"So." She sniffled. She felt done crying. "What do you

think we should do?" She held the penlight in her mouth and sifted through her papers, while she waited for his answer. He was looking at the road, driving. It was all dark. There were no attractions. "Hello?" she said.

He yawned. His face to her through the darkness in the car seemed stretched out and sagging. He was seventy-one. He'd been driving for two hours, since she'd acquiesced and they'd stopped for a burger. She hadn't wanted to stop: she wanted to get there, to be there, to face whatever it was. To help, if she could. Nan was going to be there. She admired Nan, but Nan wasn't the warmest person. Now it would be worse.

"You want me to drive?" she asked.

He nodded. The road held the dark, and there was no sign of an exit. He yawned again, loudly.

"I guess you can pull over," she said.

Immediately he pulled the car to the side of the interstate. He was spent. She opened her door.

"No, no," he lied. "I'll get out."

"It's all right," she said. She climbed from the car—it was a kind of recreation vehicle, a Montero they were leasing. It was white and rode high and you weren't supposed to take the curves and turns too tightly. She shut the door while he struggled to slide over. The night air felt cold and still. Stars were out, pointing at her. There was no moon. It was alarming how big it all felt, those stars, the vast empty land that stretched out forever into darkness. The immensity seemed to crush against her. She caught her breath. It was all so big. This enormous present. She tried to breathe deeply in it, to be as big as it was, but it was crushing. She walked around the front of the car. He had tried to open the door for her but it hung there only ajar and she had to pull it open and climb in behind the wheel and pull it shut. She was sixty-three. God she was old.

"You all right?" he said. His hand quivered as he patted her shoulder.

"I'm fine." She felt all the darkness spilling into the car. She pulled the door shut. Soon he'd be asleep, and she'd have only the glow of the dashboard for company. She reached back for the discarded lap desk and found her penlight. She clicked it on and put it in her mouth, shifted the car into drive and pulled from the side of the road.

"What are you doing?" he said.

She pulled the pen from her mouth and held it between two fingers like a cigarette as she managed the wheel. "I'm driving," she said.

"We're going to have to charge you," the detective said. Between them was a telephone and a clock radio and a full pitcher of iced water. Each of their paper cups was empty. "I don't see what choice we have."

Warner looked at him. It was nearly midnight, but his face remained crisp. They'd had a long talk, mostly about his anger—the detective had named it rage, but Warner was certain he'd made it clear that it wasn't that—and a little bit about when and where and who with. It still hadn't felt like an interrogation. It had seemed like a conversation.

"Will there be bail?"

The detective opened his hands to the question. He turned to the two-way mirror. "Henry," he said. "What do you think you'll ask for in bail?" He cupped his ear, as if sometimes he could hear Henry and sometimes he couldn't.

Warner thought he heard something. "He'll come in in a minute," the detective said. "Look." He leaned back and put his hands behind his head like a pillow. "The facts are against you. If you want to confess and if your wife survives, you won't be looking at too much. What do you say?"

"I didn't do it. I can't and I won't confess to what I didn't do."

The detective shook his head. He smiled, almost imperceptibly. "You did it. Who the heck else would do it?" He sat up straight and poured himself a glass of water. His starched white collar was knotted by a paisley tie, against the pinstripes of his gray suit. "That place didn't have a dime in it and there wasn't anybody else in the vicinity," he said. "And your alibi is you were driving around with the kids asleep in the back? Even if you can't see it yet, this is a domestic."

Warner poured himself some of the icy water. "I'll need a lawyer for the arraignment?"

"That would be wise. You want to make the call now?"

"I want my call. Yes."

The detective pushed him the telephone. For a moment, he couldn't think of a phone number, then it came to him. They'd said he could call whenever he wanted. It had been a long time. He didn't recognize the voice that answered the phone. "Mr. Lutz," the next voice bubbled, oddly cheerful, "she's still critical. Nothing's changed. We expect to know more in the morning. I guess you know her mother brought the kids in. She tolerated that without incident."

"What?"

"It went as well as could be expected."

"She brought the kids in?" Warner nearly roared.

"People do that sometimes," the nurse said calmly, "with head trauma. They think familiar voices will have an effect.

That kind of thing. But Ms. Kendall has biomedical issues. It's not just a question of her waking up."

"How'd the kids do?"

"Like I said, it went as well as could be expected. Thank you for calling, Mr. Lutz. You can call again whenever you like." She hung up. Evidently it had finally dawned on her that she'd said too much.

His hand was shaking. His head hurt. Reluctantly he gave up the phone. There were spots in his eyes. Another guy stood before him, young, younger even than him. "Would you rise, please," he said. From a weird distance the detective was watching. They all seemed suddenly leery of him, unsure of how'd he react. He just wanted to get it over with. He held out his hands, palms up, the wrists touching as if he were a supplicant. Wasn't this how it was done? "Warner Nathan Lutz," the attorney said. His ears felt filled with a kind of foam, and he could not quite hear everything. His face was flushed, his hands numb. He didn't want to look at them. He kept nodding his head, trying to speed them on, trying to assure them that he heard what he was absolutely unable to discern. Was he imagining that they were smiling? He felt too dutiful, too obliging. The attorney opened the door, and the detective's hand held an arm as they led him out into a carpeted corridor, back down the hall to where he'd come in. If only he could just step out. He had a million questions. Megan. The children. They only wanted him to snap, that's why they were so damn professional. To reveal himself. He had nothing to reveal. His fingertips were pressed into ink and then filled white forms. A light flashed in his face. In nine hours they'd tell him how much it would cost to get out of here. He took the appointed attorney. He thanked them for it.

He didn't yet have to give up what he was wearing. They took the belt from his long coat.

"You going to be okay?" the detective asked. "You look a little pale."

He nodded, his lips closed together.

"Tomorrow," the detective said.

Down another corridor, doors buzzing shut behind him, their mesh windows glaring at the back of his head as he walked with a guy in dark blue on either arm. Cinder block painted thickly white. You could still see its pores. A Christmas calendar on the wall of an office where he gave up more of himself.

"Motherfucker," someone screamed across the concrete.

TAKE CARE THAT NO ONE HATES YOU JUSTLY was one of the signs coming slowly to him in the office window, glued like bumper stickers against the wired glass. The gentleman handing out and taking in seemed to be grinning idiotically. He was an idiot.

Inside, deep inside, shut in.

Would they turn out the light?

YOU WILL MEET GOD.

FAITH DOESN'T PANIC.

They wouldn't turn out the light. The light wasn't even on.

At three—she was still awake, lying there in the living-room bed, the phone at her ear—there was a light, cautious knocking at the town-house door. She climbed from the bed and pulled on her robe. Through the peephole she could barely recognize them, their faces engulfed in shadow. She unchained the door, her heart shrinking. She hadn't expected this. She supposed she should have, but she hadn't known. He hadn't told her.

"Alan," she said. "Ruth. Come on in." She turned from them and reached for light switches along the hall and inside the kitchen, getting as many as she could. In the living room she couldn't help but feel embarrassed by the bed.

Ruth came in quickly, shivering. She stared at the bed, looked away. Alan was still coming in, shutting the door.

"How's Megan?" Ruth asked.

"Oh. Well. They don't know. I think she's going to be fine, but with head injuries they have to wait." She was clutching her thin gold necklace as she talked, strange that she'd forgotten to take it off before bed.

"Warner's at the hospital?"

Now Alan stood huffing beside Ruth, catching his breath as if they'd walked the last few miles.

"Well." Nan felt for her necklace. "He's . . . he's answering some questions up at the police station."

"Oh," Ruth said.

"What?" Alan said.

Nan remembered he had trouble hearing. "The police are asking him some questions," she said more clearly. He nodded.

Ruth stood there, looking about the living room.

"Well." Nan gripped at her necklace. "You all are welcome to stay here. I wouldn't mind getting back to the hospital. The kids are asleep. Finally. They are *so* cute. I think they've changed even since Christmas." She awkwardly patted the bed. "This has fresh sheets. Warner did them before he left. And I haven't really slept in them. You must be tired from your drive. You drove, right?"

Alan nodded. Ruth still stood there, her mouth hanging slightly open.

"I'll just get ready, then." She gathered her clothes and fled to the powder room, shut the door quickly behind her. It was very small, and she tripped over the step stool planted at the sink. She closed the toilet seat and set her clothes on it, wrestled out of her robe and nightgown. She tried not to hear whether they were talking. She didn't want to hear them stop when she pushed her way out from the tiny bathroom. She didn't want to make the situation any more uncomfortable than it already was. She ran the water in the sink. She struggled into her slacks and pullover, glanced at the big mirror, shut off the water, and opened the door. They were standing just as she had left them, looking mutely at each other, their coats still on.

"Okay," she said gaily, as if calling to a waiting companion. "Okay." She saw her keys and purse on the pass-through and snatched them up, reached into the hall closet and pulled out her overcoat and shouldered into it. Should she tell them she'd phone them or that she'd see them soon? They were looking at her. Ruth couldn't even talk, and she was a talker. "Take care," Nan said, and slid herself from the town house.

Well, she thought, that was perfectly awful. Her head seemed to depressurize, and her jaw unclenched. She walked slowly to the rental car, breathing as deeply as she could.

At the hospital, despite the thick carpeting and the newness, the blank halls had the sickly familiar hollow quality she recalled too well from her mother's death. She'd died in the middle of the night. She'd died after being rescued by ambulance and operated on by skilled surgeons and riding smoothly into recovery. She'd died after Nan had sat with her for days and then finally flown back to Atlanta, assured by her mother's doctor that she was through the worst, only to be called the next night and be told she was dead. She'd died, but she was in her eighties. Megan was in her thirties.

The ICU nurse, chipper as ever, hailed her with a "good morning." As Nan understood it, they worked twelves at this particular hospital, on the eights, they said. It must have been a cost-cutting measure, but she didn't want to say anything. You weren't supposed to aggravate the nurses. You were supposed to co-opt them. She hadn't told them yet that she was the head of fiscal planning for a national HMO. She'd been checking up on Megan's doctors. Everybody she'd called liked them, liked the facility.

She stood at the foot of the bed and looked at her daughter. A long fluorescent tube above the headboard was lit, green curtains were drawn at the large windows. She couldn't help but look a little green. Her eyes seemed to be blackening, although she'd been hit in the back of the head. The respirator was taped securely to her mouth. Her thin arms lay extended at her sides, two IV lines pumping into the back of one hand, a tube in her nose. Her heart rate seemed slow, steady, her blood pressure a bit low. Nan didn't know much about medicine, but from experience she knew enough.

"No change?" she said.

"No, ma'am."

Her daughter was attached to so many monitors and lines that Nan was afraid to touch her, those soft always slightly flushed cheeks. Nan's hand moved toward her face.

"May I?" she asked.

"Of course," said the nurse.

She'd first arrived at change of shift and hadn't even been allowed into the room. When she came with the children she'd been occupied with holding them and letting them look. Now she stroked her girl's cheek with the backs of two fingers, then touched her with two fingertips. That sweetness, the supple skin.

"Mom's here," she said, touching her. "Get better, sweetie."

She reached and stroked the other cheek, so one side wouldn't feel neglected.

"Can she hear me yet?" she asked.

"I don't think so, ma'am. But you should still talk to her."

"The kids are asleep," she said softly. "Ruth and Alan are down. You get some rest." She bent and kissed her on one cheek, right above the tape, then walked around the bed and kissed the other cheek.

A green chair sat in a corner. Maybe she shouldn't have said that thing about Ruth and Alan. She didn't want to upset her. Her signs stayed steady. Nan couldn't bring herself to sit in the green chair.

"I think I'll get a cup of coffee," she said.

"We'll be here," said the nurse.

Ruth had sensed someone waking, but when she opened her eyes it was still black. Daniel was squalling from behind his door upstairs. She thumped up the steps, opened the door, flicked on the light. He screamed at her. She took him up. He let her hold him, yowling but folding into her, clutching at her. She felt worn out. He shrieked, pushed away from her, looked beyond her through the bright light to the dark door, probably wondering where Mommy was, where Daddy was. She rocked him. Against her shoulder a knot lifted in his stomach. His mouth opened, letting it out over her shoulder onto the carpet. She didn't stop holding him. Her nightgown when he clutched her again pressed damply against her back. When she tried to set him down, he screamed. She carried him from the room and down the dark stairs. In the kitchen the light was bright, and he let her set him on the white floor. She showed him his bowl, and he cooed at it. She showed him the orange box, and he cooed again. She poured, mixed, stirred, and took him to his chair, switching the lights on as she fought her way around furniture and luggage. She set him in his chair, buckled him, clicked in the tray. The bowl between them, she lifted the blue spoon. He swallowed. She handed him the spoon. He looked at her as he ate. He swiped at her face with the spoon. She said his name. She offered him her nose. He took it and squeezed. Ow, she said. But she kept giving it to him, taking it back, giving it to him. He finished the bowl. He held the spoon and bit on it hard. She wiped his face with a clean damp towel. The bed made sounds. He saw the huge mound the body under the covers made and turned back to her bewildered.

By six-thirty Daniel was asleep and Sophie was beginning to stir. Ruth tried to count up the time she herself had slept, but it didn't even add to one hour, and she had to be at the station by nine. Warner didn't have any clothes, according to the officer she'd talked to, and he probably wanted a suit for the arraignment. Alan still slept. She wondered if it all might have been easier without him, yet she needed him to watch the kids while she was gone. He wouldn't be up to it, but she had to.

"Good morning, Sophie," she said to the girl, her eyes not quite fully open. "It's Grandma. We came for a visit."

"Where's Mommy?" Sophie yawned, tried to open her eyes, kept them shut. "Where's Granny Nan?"

"Mommy's still . . ." Ruth stopped. She didn't know what Sophie knew.

"At the hospital?" Sophie opened her eyes.

"Yes. Granny Nan's with her."

"Daddy's answering questions?"

"Yes."

She started to whimper. "I want to see Mommy."

Ruth held her. She was so thin, it was creepy. "Come on downstairs and I'll make you breakfast," she said.

Sophie held her hand as they walked down the stairs. "Is today a school day?"

It was Tuesday. It had to be. She felt a little behind the curve. She couldn't remember their routine. At least Sophie could talk! And she had to get Alan up. She had to get going.

"We'll see," she said. "Is it still oatmeal? Do you want to help me fix it?"

"Sure." Sophie trailed her into the kitchen. Ruth found the long canister of oatmeal and placed it on the floor. Sophie scooped it into a bowl, Ruth added water, and then closed it in the microwave. In two minutes, it was done. It wasn't quite seven. She had directions to the station, not twenty minutes away. She had time.

"Can we watch television?" Sophie said. "I'm allowed to watch a hour a day and it's always in the morning. See how the TV is pointed to the table."

Ruth peered through the pass-through. "I see," she said. She set the table, following Sophie's instructions for the sugar and cinnamon and a glass of milk. Sophie came and sat down, and Ruth switched the television on with the remote.

"Do you know what channel?" she asked.

"It's on the sticker on the back. We want PBS."

She turned over the remote. The numbers and letters were so small she couldn't make them out.

"Daddy!" Sophie squealed.

Ruth practically dropped the remote. When she looked up, she could see him quite clearly, stepping from a police car. "Ohhh," she said. She rushed to the television and smacked at the power button. In the bed beside her, Alan gave a soft moan, then resumed snoring.

"That was Daddy!" Sophie said. "Daddy was on television! I want to see it!"

"Sophie." Ruth came and sat at the table with her. She was standing on her seat, waiting for the television to turn back on. "It's a little early yet. There's the sugar. Help yourself."

Sophie lifted the lid from the cobalt sugar bowl and began spooning around in it. She showed her a small heap. "Is this all right?"

"Yes."

She doused her oatmeal with sugar. "Why was Daddy on television?"

"I don't know, dear. I didn't hear."

"We could turn it back on."

"It's too early, dear. Look, Pop-Pop's still asleep."

"Pop-Pop?" Sophie said. She peeked at the bed. "Oh, I didn't see." She giggled, colored in her oatmeal with cinnamon.

"That's enough," Ruth said.

She started to eat it in half-falling-off spoonfuls. "Why do you *think* Daddy was on television?" Ruth looked at her and shrugged. "Am I going to school today?"

"Probably not," she admitted.

"I want to see Mommy. And when's Granny Nan coming back?"

"I don't know, dear."

"Mommy has a lot of machines tied to her. Granny Nan showed us."

It was after seven. She was almost done with her oatmeal. "Maybe it's time to turn the television on," Ruth said.

"Okay." She gulped at her milk. "Will you call the hospital now?"

She had reached to clear the bowl, but now she stopped.

"If you don't know the number you can hit redial. Daddy and I called it all the time last night. I bet Granny Nan did, too."

She'd called the police station, she'd called Ronald in New York. She hadn't thought of calling the hospital. What *was* the matter with her? She didn't even know which hospital.

"Sophie, do you remember the hospital's name?"

"I think," Sophie shut her eyes, "it's called Memory."

In the Yellow Pages, Ruth found Memorial. She dialed the general number, asked to be put through to the ICU, and told the woman there Megan's name. "There's someone in there you can speak with," the woman said curtly.

"Wait," Ruth said.

The phone rang again.

"Hello?" It was Nan.

"Hi, Nan," Ruth said weakly. "It's Ruth. Sophie—we—wanted to know how it was going."

"Same as before. I think we'll hear more when they do the rounds. Could you put Sophie on?"

She moved with the cordless out to the table, where Sophie sat eating her oatmeal.

"Granny Nan wants to talk to you," she said.

The girl dropped her spoon in the bowl and reached for the phone. "Hello, Granny Nan?" she said. She smiled as she listened. "Why can't I talk to her?" Her face fell a little, but she nodded her head. Ruth patted her shoulder, and she shrugged it off. "When will I see you?" she asked. She listened intently and smiled. "Okay. Bye." She handed the phone to Ruth. "She's going to take me shopping today," she said.

"Nan?" Ruth said in the receiver.

The line was empty.

"I guess she had to go," she said, shutting off the cordless.

"She said Mommy's getting better." Sophie tried to smile. "She said Mommy's resting. That's why she can't talk."

"I see," Ruth said.

"Can I watch television now? We can't call again for a hour, I think."

"Absolutely." Ruth got her glasses and read the channel numbers, turned on PBS, turned up the sound. Sophie sat at the table watching.

"I'm going to get dressed," Ruth said.

"All right. When do you think Pop-Pop will get up?"

"I'll wake him soon."

In the tight powder room she got back into her office clothes because she was going to the arraignment and she supposed that this was how you dressed when your son was getting arraigned. Ronald had said that they'd definitely set a reasonable bail, although it was not his field of specialty. She hadn't called any of the other kids, and she hadn't asked him to. She wanted to wait. She couldn't bear it. She wished Alan would wake up.

For reasons she could not quite discern the medical staff were beginning to drop in and out of her daughter's room. It was something about Megan's pupils in conjunction with the blood pressure. The pictures were supposed to be conclusive, but perhaps they weren't. Nan couldn't pick up everything, and she didn't want to interrupt. She pressed herself against the wall and tried to understand.

The pupils were no longer equal in size. The brain's pressure on the skull seemed to be in ascent. The numbers that mattered were up. The head nurse called the OR. The OR was free.

"Thirty minutes," said a middle-aged man in green, looking past Nan to nurses tapping new wires into Megan. "We'll shave her here."

"Excuse me?" Nan said.

"That's the mother," another nurse said.

"Dr. Lyons." The doctor extended his hand, shook hers. "As you've no doubt heard, your daughter is destabilizing. We're going to have to relieve some of the pressure caused by the swelling of her brain. It will be a relatively simply procedure."

"I thought she was stable," Nan said. She felt herself clutching her necklace, but she didn't care.

"These situations can be fluid. The brain is suspended in liquid, and when there is external trauma, it can get knocked around against the sides of the skull, injuring the tissue. There were three—perhaps more—traumatic events to your daughter's brain. While her numbers were stable, we could regard her situation as stable, but her situation has always been uncertain. The numbers we have now indicate that the brain is swelling and putting too much pressure on the skull. We need to reduce some of that pressure."

"Brain surgery?" Nan found herself nearly ripping off her necklace.

"Not quite. We're going to open up a bit more breathing space for the brain by taking a bit more out of the skull."

"But the doctors last night said . . ."

"Ma'am, your daughter's situation has changed."

At the bedside an electric razor began to drone. Nan pointed to it.

"Don't you generally do that in the OR? Isn't the fact that the back of her head is already shaved enough? Shouldn't this all wait?"

"No, ma'am. Katy?" A nurse appeared. "Why don't you take Mrs. Kendall down to OR waiting? We'll all be along shortly."

Katy began to firmly lead her from the room.

"Don't you . . ." Nan twisted just as firmly but she hoped not ridiculously in her grip. "Don't you need me to sign something?"

"Oh no, ma'am," the neurosurgeon called after her. "Her husband did."

"But—" But she was out the door, and the door was shut, and through the window she could see them shaving Megan's head. "This is a new surgery," she heard herself saying. "I don't even know this guy. I don't know if he's any good."

"He's very good, Mrs. Kendall," Katy said crisply.

"Really." She looked at Katy. That scrubbed, unblemished face. A year out of nursing school at most. "I need to make some phone calls. I'm sure I can find the waiting room myself."

She ducked into an empty rest room and pulled out her cell phone and electronic Rolodex. Eight o'clock. Everybody would be in transit. The signed release by the accused assailant was a legal issue with which she had absolutely no familiarity. It sounded like Von Bulow territory. Her staff wasn't due in until eight-thirty, her legal and medical sources at Corporate often didn't arrive before nine. She stared at the blank screen of her Rolodex. She should have anticipated the potential restraining order, her guardianship over both Megan and the children. With a sudden horror she realized that she herself was supposed to be at Corporate by ten for a management team meeting with the CEO. She reached into a stall and snatched at a roll of soft tissue. She didn't *need* to cry. She was crying. They were going to open up her skull even more. It could draw a line between who she was and who she would be afterward. Could she die? She couldn't die. You didn't outlive your children. That was absurd. She was weeping. The door opened, and she looked up with bits of tissue sticking to her face and there was Katy looking at her.

"Your daughter's outside," she said softly. "If you want to . . ."

"Yes," she sniffled. "Yes, thank you. Everything's happening so fast."

"It can sometimes," Katy said in what struck her as a profoundly gentle way, holding open the door.

Nan wiped at her face and went out. In the still hall her daughter's head was shaved, her eyes shut inside darkened rings of skin. Her face was white, and her mouth seemed to take in the respirator in a sucking manner. "Oh, sweetie," Nan said, kissing her on the cheek. "You're going to be okay, sweetie. I'll see you so soon." She lay remote on the gurney. She began to roll away. Nan's lips brushed her cheek. The gurney clanked past. Nan dabbed at her eyes. Now she was alone in the wide hall.

When his old gray suit came into the cell he shook his head without words and marveled at his mother, somewhere out there beyond the walls, who had saved him again. Who was always saving him. Why couldn't he remember that whenever he felt all that hate for her, all that impatience, all that superiority? His head ached from the lack of alcohol the previous night, and he felt dizzy. He hadn't eaten in a while. He hadn't really slept.

He picked up the suit. Inside a jacket sleeve his mother had stuffed a neatly rolled-up pair of boxers and black socks. A pair of dress shoes were in an accompanying plastic bag. He thanked the officer and waited for him to leave. He began to dress, his back to the window. As he was buckling his pants there was a knock at the door. He turned. A woman with short brown hair parted in the middle waved at him. The door opened, and she strode in. Even in high heels she was shorter, slight. She wore brown.

"Polly Edwards," she said, shaking his hand. "Your court-appointed attorney."

"We're meeting in here?" he said.

"Sometimes things get a little backed up." She didn't really smile; she kept a fixed near-friendly expression. "How are you going to plead?"

"Not guilty."

"Well, wait a minute. I need to tell you the situation. Your wife's in surgery. She's iffy—"

"Ohhh," he moaned. He knew she was critical. He knew the kids were without them. He knew today he was losing his job. He knew that the house was over. But through the night, as he dipped near and away from sleep, he'd wondered in abstractions—what kind of husband he was, what kind of father, what kind of son, what kind of brother. He hadn't thought his way out. He hadn't thought.

"I'm innocent," he said.

She looked at him. She wasn't anywhere near southern, and she looked him in the eyes and tried to tell.

"Okay," she said matter-of-factly. "We can always change it, but it will only be worse."

"Thank you," he said dryly.

"Bail will be anywhere between one hundred thousand and a million."

That knocked the wind out of him. He felt how cold his sockless feet were.

"If you can meet ten percent, then the rest can be arranged."

Numbly he nodded. "Do you have a pen? Paper?"

She handed him both, and he explained to her as he began to write a note to his mother.

"Have you told her yet?"

"No." She pressed her lips together, as if trying to assimilate the fact that he had a mother. "You can assume there will be some kind of restraining order. Getting out on bail won't mean going home."

"Okay, okay." He was beginning to feel a little clobbered.

"So the family's all in," she said, in a way that made it sound like they'd arrived for a wedding. He didn't reply; he was still writing his mother instructions for accessing their savings account. He gave her the note. "Well," she said awkwardly. "I'm glad we've met. I'll see you in an hour or so." She tapped on the door and was released.

His head throbbed. So she didn't believe him. Who the hell would? He knocked on the door and asked to use a phone. He was politely denied. Quickly he pulled on his socks and tied his shoes, buttoned the collar of his shirt and knotted his tie, drew on his jacket. He was glad there was no mirror. His breakfast sat on a plastic tray. Corn flakes in milk, a banana, a glass of juice, a room-temperature cup of coffee. Again he tried the coffee. It was colder. He made himself drink it. It was thin and metallic and inoffensive. His window was empty. He waited.

On the sofa Pop-Pop was joggling Daniel. Daniel bawled. Pop-Pop looked at her almost for advice. He was too fat to get off the sofa with Daniel on him. Maybe he was too fat to do anything.

"Is it a hour yet?" she asked.

"What?" Pop-Pop said. Pop-Pop was hard of hearing.

"A hour," she shouted. "I want to call Mommy."

Pop-Pop tried to set Daniel beside him. Daniel wriggled and cried. He looked sweaty. Beside him Pop-Pop picked up the phone and hit the redial button, his face baggy. Daniel shrieked or was still. His high-chair tray lay on the floor between them. She was sitting cross-legged, listening hard through Daniel. "What?" Pop-Pop was saying. "What?"

"Let me talk," she said.

He shook his head hard and slapped at the air. He was sour. Daniel's diaper smelled. Pop-Pop was really old. He'd had a lot of operations. He was sick. She didn't let herself talk while he held the phone tight to his head and tried to amuse Daniel with his fat fingers. Finally, he hung up. He looked sad.

"No news yet, Sophie," he said, his voice groggy and choked. "I'm sorry."

"That's all right," she said. She picked up a doll and held it. "We can call in a hour."

With all his might Pop-Pop lifted Daniel from the sofa and placed him carefully on the floor. Then Pop-Pop got down on the floor beside him, down on his belly. Daniel swatted at him, smiled, and began to crawl on Pop-Pop's back. Pop-Pop was a mountain on the floor. He groaned happily. She rested her doll and drew near. He was sweet on the floor like that, smiling and cooing through the smell of Daniel's diaper, his face round and fat and bald. He could have been Santa. He could have been a clown. She was glad he was Pop-Pop.

Nan worked the phone all morning, checking on Lyons, the restraining order, the outcome of the arraignment, possible guardianship, the management team meeting, and why the flowers she had ordered had never arrived. Around her the waiting room filled with anxious mothers and fathers and daughters and sons and assorted relatives awaiting news from the operating suite. She talked into the receiver in a low, precise voice and the others read or worked on laptops or gazed distractedly at magazines. There was no television.

Warner had been assessed $400,000 in bail and instructed that he could not at this time reside with the children or be within one thousand feet of them without the presence of one of the three court-appointed adults—herself and his parents. He was in any case not to visit or see or speak to his wife. She heard he was in the process of leveraging funds for the bail. She had tried to freeze their savings, but he'd got what he needed and the rest wouldn't take more than a few hours. At the expense of the embarrassment of her explaining the reason, she'd been excused from the management team meeting. The florist would credit her account for the undelivered flowers. From the operating suite came no word of her daughter. Whenever Nan stopped talking on the phone, she felt overwhelmed with panic. In her Rolodex she searched for more people to call.

She tried to remember a time when she was unconscious, years ago when they'd taken out her appendix. Under anesthesia there was only darkness, separation, no process, nothing beyond or between. It was only time lost. Or gone: time gone. She'd woken up and thought it hadn't even happened yet, until she felt the actual pain. Then she knew it had happened and she had somehow missed it. Megan was missing it. That was a comfort, to know at this point, under anesthesia, she wasn't enduring anything. She was not a part of it. She was missing it.

Was the color of being anesthetized black or white? She thought it black, deep, like Frost's woods. Not like Eliot's yellow. It had been a long time since she'd thought like this. Now she read whatever was on the Oprah list, even though she didn't watch Oprah. She went to movies and restaurants alone, or with couples. At night, if she was lucky, she'd be home in Buckhead with a Bailey's on ice, reading, perhaps a little paperwork, a call to Megan before bed. That was her routine. She tried not to call every day. Some days she couldn't help it. She wasn't traveling, she'd had Bailey's, the suburban house was big and empty, the phone was in her hand. Weeks could go by like that. Other weeks she'd be at a conference, or on those long vacations she made herself take—arctic cruises, Southeast Asian swings, adult tennis camps—and she couldn't call, and Megan's sense of relief across all that silence seemed palpable to her.

She rested the phone in her lap and held her hands together. Whenever she was nervous she liked to sit like this, one hand holding the other, the four fingers of the right hand caught by the thumb and index finger of the left hand, each hand wrapped around the other; they had to meet exactly the same way each time. When she was younger she did it because her college roommates always joked about how she waved her hands whenever she got too excited at parties, then she did it to keep looking professional at all the meetings she had to attend and during all the presentations she had to give, and now she held tight to herself whenever she felt a loss of control. It no longer happened at work, never happened on vacations. She thought it only happened with Megan, or when she was thinking about Megan. Megan had tried to tease her out of it; she even would reach across and try to unglue one hand from the other. Finally she had quit saying anything. A tic. A standard ploy to keep yourself from giving your nerves away. No big deal. Was it so bad to sit quietly and clasp your hands together? Her therapist had told her it meant that she was her own best source of strength. Megan had said that she was just stepping on herself. If it was the one aftereffect of her horrible marriage and her unsatisfactory history with men, it was worth it. How long had it been since she had *really* kissed anybody? How long had she—successful, good-looking—been alone? She was aware she was losing sensation in both hands. Her thumbs and her knuckles were white. Soon they would stop. Soon she could take one hand from the other and figure out what to do next.

"Mrs. Kendall?" She looked up at Dr. Lyons, his face drawn and serious. He knelt beside her like some kind of sideline coach. "We were able to relieve the pressure on Megan's skull." He let a brief smile escape. "She's still comatose. We'll need to see how she is when she wakes up."

"And that will be?"

"We don't know." He shook his head. "It's always hard to tell in these cases. We did the best we could."

She restrained herself in this river of clichés. "Is there any permanent damage?"

"We don't believe so, but that's still hard to say."

"What about the need for further surgery?" She was beginning to hate him, how careful he was. Of course he had to be careful in what he said, but she just wanted to shake him and make him tell her what he truly thought.

"We'd prefer not to conjecture at this point. Again, what we can tell you, all we can really tell you," he stood, folding his arms across his chest, "is that the pressure on her skull has been relieved. Do you have any questions?"

"How long can you stay?" He tried to project gratitude in his voice, and he looked at her squarely as she glanced over from her driving. He tried to show her how grateful he was, how ashamed he was, how penitent. Whatever it took, he wanted to show her. He hoped they wouldn't have to talk about it.

"I was thinking," she said, her eyes back on the road, her fingertips tapping the wheel. "I was thinking maybe I would fly back and Dad would stay. That would allow you to go see the kids whenever you wanted. And he'd be good company."

"Does he want to?" How crisp everything now seemed to him: the black asphalt of the road, the winter brownness of the trees, the red and green of the stoplights. The world was so damn crisp. He'd almost lost it. "I mean." He groped for words, gave it up. "You know what I mean."

"If you asked him. You'd have to ask him."

"It'd be a lot easier than dealing one-on-one with Nan." He felt her look at him sharply. "I mean, I'd love for Dad to stay."

"You two could get a hotel room somewhere. You could start working on your defense. He could talk with Nan about a schedule for you to see the kids. It wouldn't be so bad."

"You've got it all figured out." He grinned.

"Is it straight or to the left here?" she said, pointing at the intersection.

"Straight."

"I can't just drop my work," she said. "You know that." He nodded. "I don't want you to."

"Is there anything you want to say?"

"No." He swallowed. "I'm so glad you came down. I needed you to be here and you came. What else can I say?"

"Did you do it?" she said.

"What?"

"Did you do it? I won't tell anybody, but I need to know." She reached under her glasses and blotted her eyes. He hadn't seen her cry in a long time. "As your mother," she said, "I have a right."

"I didn't do it," he said.

"Come on, Warner." She was practically sobbing. "Who else would do it."

"I don't know, Mom. I really don't know. But I didn't do it. I hit her once, okay? That was exactly ten years ago. I've gone over all that with the police."

"Why'd you hit her?" she sobbed. She was struggling to compose herself. She had to keep driving.

He sighed. "I don't really want to go into it."

"Go into it!" she screamed.

"All right. All right." He couldn't look at her. He looked out the window. Myers Park, again. You couldn't escape Myers Park. It was there, in your face, on the way to the station, on the way to court, on the way to places to eat, on the way uptown, on the way to work. Its fat hand had cupped a place between Crape Myrtle Hill and everything he wanted or had to do. Fucking Myers Park. The hell with Myers Park. "It was New Year's Eve," he said to the window, to the neighborhood. "I'd spent the night before with you guys. She'd spent it with Nan. So I drive all the way down there for New Year's Eve, and she's weird, kind of distant. We go out to dinner with two of her friends." He kept looking out the window. "I knew something was weird. When I'd come down, Nan had given me a kind of strange—I don't know, *sympathetic*—look. Nan doesn't parcel out sympathy all that well. She tends to believe that whatever you get, you've done it to yourself. It's your fault. She's very Calvinist that way. You get cancer; it's your fault. You break your leg; it's your fault. You don't make enough money; it's your fault. I guess I kind of hate her." He gave a little gulp at that. "Anyway, after dinner, which ended about eight, Megan insists we go back to her mom's house. She says she's tired, kind of hungover. That should have been a clue. We get to her mom's house—Nan's house—whatever—and we're standing in the foyer and she says, I have to tell you something. I went out with Mike last night—Mike was her fiancé prior to me—and I spent the night with him. You what? I said. I mean, it's New Year's Eve, I'm living with this woman, have been living with her for *six months,* going out with her for more than two years, and she's telling me she slept with her former fiancé. On New Year's Eve. In her mother's house, she's telling me this." He felt afraid of the rage he was hearing in his own voice, but he had to keep going; she wanted to hear it. She'd asked. "And I pull back my hand. I remember pulling it back, like it had a tennis racket or something. And I slapped her face. And she's crying and backing away from me, and I reach to slap her face again and maybe I connect, I'm not sure this time. And I try one last time—three times in all—and then I'm done." He pointed at the window. "Listen to how young I sound. It was ten years ago, for Christ's sake."

"I'm just listening," his mother sniffled. "I'm just listening to how *mad* you sound."

"I'm not mad," he said, feeling horror as the words escaped him. "I got even."

"How?" she said.

"I went and slept with somebody, too."

"That's sick," she said. "You are sick."

"It was ten years ago," he said. "I'm over it."

"No you're not," she said.

He looked back at her then. Her face had such an edge. "I guess you told Dad I hit you."

"I guess I did."

"I was eleven years old, Mom. Goddamn it, I was eleven years old."

"And you were twenty-five when you hit Megan. And you're thirty-five now. So what."

"It's up there," he said, pointing to the wide-mouthed driveway into Crape Myrtle Hill.

"I know," she said. "Believe me, I know." She veered abruptly into the drive, her face rippling. "I guess you're thinking about how *I* hit *you*," she said, making herself drive slowly.

"I'm not."

"I know you think about it."

"I have." He couldn't quite believe they were talking this way.

She pulled into a parking place, yanked the emergency brake. "Your brother and sisters never talk about it. They never mention they think about it. Not a word. They love me."

"I love you, too." He tried to touch her. She flinched. "Even if you hit me more."

She glanced at him, her eyes pooled behind her glasses. "Obviously," she said, "I didn't hit you enough."

"Jesus." He coughed out a laugh. It was so hollow it actually hurt. He couldn't understand and yet he did understand why they were having this conversation.

"If you use this for your defense," she said, shaking her head, not quite ready to open the door, "that is really sick."

He looked at her horrified. It had never occurred to him. "Mom," he said, "I didn't do it."

"Right," she said. She slammed out of the car.

Almost reluctantly he followed her toward the town house. He marched in and Daniel looked up from the floor and started crying, and Sophie came skipping from the sofa and sailed into his legs and said, "Daddy, you're back," and his father eyed him from the bed where he slumped, sagging, with a mix of expressions none of which seemed welcoming. Warner lifted Sophie up and hugged her, nuzzled in her neck.

"Oh, sweetie," he murmured.

He carried her over to where Daniel sat paralyzed in tears and set her down and scooped him up, and Daniel bawled against his shoulder, his little chest stiff. Warner rocked him and rocked him, but he kept crying.

"He was fine until you came in," his father said.

"Honey," Warner said, "honey. Do you want something to eat?" He carried him toward the kitchen, bumping past his mom, Sophie clinging to a leg. In the freezer he found a wheel of frozen waffle and snapped off a piece, and Daniel said, "Hmmm?" and took it and began to gnaw at it, his face composing.

"Me, too," Sophie said.

"A frozen waffle?"

She nodded.

He gave her a wedge and he stood with them there in the ten-foot kitchen, Sophie holding on to his knee, Daniel nibbling at the waffle and patting at his daddy's back. Warner could have stayed in the kitchen like that for a good long while. He walked out to the living room.

His mother was dumping papers into tote bags and setting them on her lap desk by the stairs. His father was still sitting on the bed, feet on the floor, hands balled into fists at his side as if he might rise.

"What's up," Warner said.

"I gotta get going." His mother looked tersely at him.

"Well." Warner told himself to breathe once, breathed once. "Do you have a reservation?"

"I'm driving," she said. "You two don't need two cars."

"It's five hundred miles. It'll take all night."

"I like driving at night," she said.

"I do, too," Sophie said.

His mother smiled at her. "Do you want to come?"

The girl shook her head fiercely, buried her face in Warner's thigh.

"I'm sorry," Warner said.

"About what?" She glanced at him with innocence and a look of interrogation.

"Everything." He attempted to set Daniel down, but he curled like a shrimp and Warner had to keep holding him. "I didn't *want* to be having that conversation in the car."

"Nobody," his mother stared at him, her lips disappearing, her eyes brimming, "*wants* to be having *any* of these 'conversations.'" Her back to him, she pushed the tote-bag-laden lap desk toward the door.

"Then I'm sorry for everything I said," he tried. She still wouldn't look at him. "Everything I've said and done?"

She brushed past him and stood in front of his father at the bed. "Take care of yourself," she said, kissing him on his head. "Remember your pills." Around Warner, she kissed Daniel and then Sophie, strode to the door, slung a tote bag over each shoulder, and plucked up the lap desk. She looked at Warner one last time and shook her head. "You know," she said, "you and Megan aren't the only ones in this." When she left, she softly shut the door behind her.

"Wow," Warner said.

From the bed his father cleared his throat, angrily, disdainfully. "She knew she wasn't wanted," he growled. Wearily he rose and stepped past them toward the bathroom. He took in Warner once, from head to toe, looked him slowly in the eye, and shook his head. Like his mother had done. "You oughtta know," he said, his voice gravelly, "I'm only staying because she asked me to."

Alone for the moment, his father interred in the bathroom, Warner set Daniel on the floor, where he cooed and hummed. Sophie tugged at his jacket. She looked at him shyly, the room still.

"Daddy?" she said.

"Yes, sweetheart?" Her eyes seemed strangely fearful or conflicted.

"Daddy." She timidly touched his pant leg, his coat hem. "Daddy, I like your suit."

With a sickening astonishment he realized that it was himself who made her afraid. Someone must have said something. He lifted her up. She was such a big person compared to Daniel, oversize, offering these compliments to keep him at bay.

"I'm so glad to see you again," he said gently.

"Daddy." She carefully stroked his tie; her eyelids lowered against his gaze. "I like your tie." She seemed almost to be trembling.

Exposure

Water. God she was thirsty. Damn thing she was talking around. Pipe. Tube. Water. Water.

Her eyes said it was night. Her throat closed around this thing. She wanted it to open. She was parched. Sore. She wanted water. Water!

"Can you hear me?"

What was it?

"You keep saying 'Wa wa. Wa wa.' We can't give you water, honey. Not yet. They have to take out the ventilator first."

Did they have to talk so loud?

"I'll run and get permission for ice chips. Should I do that?"

She tried to nod her head furiously. She couldn't really do it. She tried to say yes.

"Okay, okay. I'm going. Oh honey, you've been asleep such a long time."

. . .

Was that Dad?

"Honey, it's the doctor. Though you're right." She heard nervous laughter. "There is kind of a resemblance."

"Megan, hey. I'm Dr. Lyons. We're going to take that tube out in just a minute. Can you hear what I'm saying? Move your fingers to tell me. That's the best way. You probably don't want to move your head too much. You can hear me? Good. Do you know you're in a hospital? Good. Do you know this is your mother? Good. Listen." He touched his hand on hers. "We'll talk more when the tube is out. You should try to get some rest." He left.

"Honey?"

She tried to make a face to tell her mom how tired she was.

"Honey." Her voice was low, knowing she shouldn't be talking, knowing she shouldn't ask. "Do you remember anything?"

What was there to forget?

"Good, honey. That's good." She gave a whispered kiss. "Get some rest. We'll talk."

"I'm not supposed to call you," she said, her voice tenuous, tender, muffled, like it had to rise to the occasion of each new word.

"It's you," he said. He'd heard she was awake; his father had told him, his eyes measuring each tremor of emotion. How was he supposed to react? What he felt was sheer relief. He pushed or fell into his father's arms, tears starting or squeezing out, the children staring from the floor, his father refusing to hold him. What days they'd had. Five days with the children in the town house, five nights at the Quality Inn, the job gone, the house and earnest money gone, the news-papers carrying the story—KENDALL WOMAN UNLIKELY TO REMEMBER, GREED AND RAGE IN CRAPE MYRTLE HILL. The attorney badgering him to plea-bargain now. Now she was awake. Now they were talking. "It's you," he tried again, his voice crumbling. It was her. He felt ready to weep like an idiot.

"Why," she said so slowly, "am I not supposed to call you."

"Oh honey," he said. "Honey." He swallowed the dryness in his throat. "I can't talk to you, honey. I can't. I'm sorry. Honey, I'm so sorry. The children—"

"The children?" she said.

"They're on their way."

"Yes. I know."

It was painful to listen to how careful her voice was, each word a step on some high wire, a breath that might not finish.

"We can't talk," he said. "We're not allowed."

"Just tell me."

"I can't. Honey, I just can't."

"Did you?" she said, with a slow sharpness that stunned him.

"Megan," he said.

His father came out of the bathroom, his pants unbuck-led. The line was cut off. He looked at the phone. Had she hung up? Had he?

"That was her?" his father growled, reaching for the phone. Warner gave it up. "You're not supposed to talk to her. You know that. Don't be dumb."

"She called," he said weakly.

"We're not even supposed to be here. Come on." He buckled his pants, moved more quickly to the door. Each day he seemed a little quicker. "We gotta go."

In the car, his father driving, he looked down at his

shoes, trying to think. She was awake. She could talk. She talked to him. Unbelievable.

"Is that why you wanted to stay?" his father said. "You knew she might call? Tell me."

"Yes," he said. "I think so."

"Don't you know?" his father snorted.

"I don't know anything anymore." The skin on his arm began to itch, and he pinched it. He ought to go see her. He wanted to see her. He could try.

"Please don't do anything stupid," his father said. "Your mother and I, we've really put ourselves out for you this time. Don't be dumb."

"Right," he said, not looking at him.

"So what did she say?"

Warner told him everything. His dad nodded and drove. Some hours when they were without the children all they did was drive around.

"Well," he said. "And not that you care what I think. I know that. Don't worry, it doesn't bother me anymore." His eyes flashed briefly. "Though it should bother you. Don't write her, don't try to visit her, don't call her, don't allow yourself to be called by her. You just have to wait. Be patient. See what happens."

"Hmmm." Warner stared at the stoplight.

"You try to go see her, it'll get misinterpreted. You write her, they'll find a way to use it. That's what I think."

"But if I don't do anything? Won't that look . . ." Warner shook his head.

"Just take care of the kids. Do what you've been doing. Call your brother. See what he says."

He wasn't going to call his brother. It was bad enough, this weird infantilization, having to have his father with him.

It was bad enough getting the phone call from work, Monique telling him, "Richard needs to talk to you," and Warner having to say, "I'll make it easy for him. I'll send a letter." It was bad enough not having a job, not having a shred of savings, the checking account dribbling to nothing. The waiting for his turn to see the kids, the awful falseness of Nan as she rushed out the door, the breezy cheerfulness of her return, her eyes narrowing in suspicion. At least she trusted his father.

He was so set aside, set off, from his own life, as if he stood on a corner while his life and everything that mattered to him was happening inside a house set back from the street. And he had to stay on that corner. He wasn't supposed to budge from it.

"I need to go see her," he said. "It's Megan, for Christ's sake."

"Doesn't matter. Wouldn't matter if it were your mother," his father turned to him and said harshly, "and you were accused of trying to murder her. Wouldn't matter if it were me. Or your brother. Or one of your sisters. Until they say you can, you are going to have to stay away."

"What if," he tried, "what if she requests it?"

"I don't know anything about that," he shrugged, "but I wouldn't count on it. Especially with Nan around. She'd get Megan ruled mentally incompetent or something."

"Fuck Nan," Warner snapped.

"Yeah," his father said with empathy. "I know what you mean."

"You what?" she said.

"I called him," Megan admitted, Daniel trying to reach under her hospital gown.

"Mommy," Sophie cooed, snuggled into her side. "Are you guys talking about Daddy?"

"He did this to you," Nan said.

"Mom, we don't *know* that. I don't know that." She felt tired, caved in, but what a relief it was to be able to talk, to interact, to go to the bathroom. To have the kids crawling all over her. "Please don't do this now."

"The fingerprints on the hammer. Your fighting shortly beforehand. Nothing missing from the gallery. No sign of anybody else even in there. His history." Nan counted out each element with a finger. "What more do you need?"

"Look. I'm tired. I'm confused. Why don't you go down to the cafeteria for a little bit." She wrestled Daniel in her arms, and he giggled. "I can handle these guys."

"I'm so glad you're awake, honey," Nan said, making herself leave. "But if I have to, I'll have them take out that phone." She tried to snap the door shut, but it was hydraulic and wouldn't close. She gave it a look and marched out.

"Granny Nan is cranky," Sophie said. "Mommy, what was it like?"

"What, honey?"

"Being asleep so long."

She sighed. She felt so sleepy. At least she knew what it was from. "It was like nothing, honey. It was just like being asleep. But I don't think I dreamed."

"I had bad dreams," Sophie said. "I haven't been to school all week."

"I'll bet." She held Daniel close, and he was still the way he was when he was thinking of a nap or he just woke up—a comforted stillness, his contented solid weight sunk into her. Sophie folded herself in as close as she could.

"I missed you," she said.

"I missed you, too."

Sophie laughed. "You were asleep. You couldn't miss anybody."

"Well, when I woke up then. Honey, don't hold me so tight. It hurts."

Sophie whimpered and withdrew.

"I'm sorry, sweetie. It's going to take me a little time."

"Is Daddy going to jail for whacking you?"

"Honey, listen." She set Daniel on her lap and reached for Sophie, held her by her arms. "I don't know what happened. I don't know what will happen. So I can't really say what I think will happen."

"Are you going to let Daddy see you?"

"I think so," she said. "We'll have to wait and see."

"Sort of like with you," Sophie decided. "That's what everybody kept saying about you. We'll have to wait and see. We'll have to wait and see. Wait and see is boring." She looked away toward the wall. "Does your TV work?"

"I don't know. Probably TV isn't such a good idea for me right now."

"Because you might see Daddy?"

"No, sweetie. Because I'm so sleepy and all the sound and pictures kind of get to me."

"Do me and Daniel kind of get to you?"

"I don't think so, honey."

"But we could, right? If we jumped up and down and made a lot of noise and shouted and stuff. That could get to you. Right?"

"Do you want to get to me?"

"No," Sophie said. "How long have you been awake, Mommy?"

"Almost two days, I think."

"You've been awake for two whole days? You haven't slept at all?"

"No, no. I've slept. I've slept off and on. And I slept for most of the night."

"Were you afraid you wouldn't wake up?"

Megan sighed. "Don't ask so many questions, honey. Okay?"

She sank deep into the pillow and let the children control the bed. Soon she heard the television click on, but she couldn't lift her eyes. She couldn't see. Her head felt heavy, pointed, and she knew she should call the nurse, but Daniel had the control and she couldn't seem to reach it. Just reach it, she thought. Just lift your hand. It weighed too much, attached to her wrist like that, anchored to her arm, her shoulder glued in its socket. Just move. Oh god, she was tired. Maybe it was the kids, the way they took it from you, the way they'd been taking it from you from the start, from that first moment inside. She'd come back too fast. Two days wasn't very fast. But they'd said it was fast. Warp speed. They looked warped, their heads softening through her eyelids. It wouldn't be good to drift off like this, with the children here. Her mother would disconnect the phone. She'd be disconnected. She *was* disconnected, something between herself and everyone else, and it was the back of her head. She couldn't see. She was drifting off. Drifting. Ring the bell. He could fall off the bed if she didn't stay awake. Stay awake. He was moving to the edge. She could feel it. Ring the bell. Mommy, someone was saying. Mommy.

· · ·

"There she is."

"Yeah."

"Keep going."

"Uh-hunh."

"Excellent."

"Yes."

"It was just the epi drip?"

"Yes."

"Good catch."

"Of course I was right here."

"Guess she wasn't ready for the kids. Where are they?"

"Outside."

"Good, good. Never again, okay? Tell them never again, the kids alone like that."

"Right. Right. I'll let everybody know."

"They couldn't know."

"Well. They could have."

"Okay. Okay. They could have."

"Ms. Kendall, if you can hear me, move your fingers. Excellent. Excellent. You're coming around nicely, Ms. Kendall. You'll be back to where you were in no time."

"So they were just in here alone like that, hunh?"

"Yeah."

"She d-c'd herself as smooth as any nurse."

"Uh-hunh."

"Tie it like that?"

"Yeah. Ankles and wrists."

"Here she is."

"Hey, Ms. Kendall. I bet that was interesting."

"We lost your epi drip there for a moment. But we're all set now."

"We're going to give you a bit of space now, okay? You're all secure. Do you understand?"

She wriggled her finger.

"Good. We'll let you rest. Okay? You can rest. It's perfectly safe. Let's let that epinephrine catch you up. Okay?"

"Okay." Faintly, but there it was. Her voice.

"Take care."

But she couldn't open her eyes. She couldn't seem to move her arms. She was too tired. There was probably nothing to see or reach. She didn't want to see or touch it anyway. That was close enough, a close call. She shouldn't have called him. What had he done? What hadn't he? Warn her. Warner. Every word was new the first time you said it again. You.

"Don't you want anything to eat?"

"No." Warner shook his head.

"I can't remember the last time I saw you eat. You haven't eaten in what? A couple of days?"

"I'm not hungry," he said.

"You have to eat." His father took a large bite from his reuben, the fleshy pink of the Thousand Island dressing oozing out against the white skin of the napkin. The layers of purple meat.

"I know," Warner said.

"When you don't eat," his father said, chewing, "you know what happens? Your stomach gets smaller and smaller. Shrinks until it's probably the size of a pea. And then you don't ever want to eat. And then you can't eat. And then, you know what?"

"What?"

"It's too late." His father smiled happily over the sandwich. "You've got to want to eat, Warner. Eating's a good thing. It can keep you going."

They sat in the car in the parking lot outside the deli, both of them listening to the satisfying crunch of his chew.

"They were talking about you on some radio show this morning," his father said with a full mouth. "How does everybody down here know you're Jewish?"

"When did Nan say she'd bring the kids back?"

He shrugged, still chewing. "She didn't." He swallowed with some finality, wiped his mouth with the tail of the napkin, took a swig of root beer. Warner had grown up in a house placarded with health ads that his mother had torn from magazines. *Eat to live, don't live to eat. That belly will kill him before he's fifty-five.* He'd learned to feel revulsion watching his father eat. "What do you want to do?" his father said, folding up the detritus and storing it in the paper bag. "I'm easy."

"You could call the hospital, find out what's going on, make a plan for later. I'd like to see the kids later."

"I could do that." He began to squeeze his belly out from behind the steering wheel. The door pushed open.

Warner pointed at the oversize chain bookstore at the corner of the shopping center. "We could meet in there."

"Okay."

He watched his father lumber toward the pay phone, then got out of the car, locked it. The day was sunny and warm on his back, nearly spring weather to him. Outside at the massive Harris Teeter they were cooking lamb sandwiches on an open grill.

In the bookstore he paged through various home medical guides. He should have done this earlier, but his father had been with him virtually constantly, and he knew it could look unsavory. Of course there was nothing in them that he hadn't read in the newspapers. The steaming arm of an espresso machine whined from the café. He wished he could talk to her. He wished he could talk to her doctors. Everything he learned was from Nan through his father. She would recover. It was all good. Polly Edwards felt "relieved" for him. He might be looking at five years or three years or even less, if he plea-bargained. Would she testify? What could she say? That he was angry, that he had a temper, that he'd hit her once? It was doubtful how much of the day's argument she would remember. It was doubtful, he knew, that she'd testify. He hadn't told Polly, but he knew. He knew that she wouldn't testify, that there'd be no trial, no case, that he'd never plea-bargain. If a trial could somehow clear him, he'd beg her to testify, but it couldn't. It wasn't "he said, she said." It was "he said, she had nothing to say." So what would happen now? Could they live together again? Did he even want that? Did she? How would he earn money? Not here, not ever. He couldn't see a place where they could live next. He had little sense of the real future. Maybe, finally, his want had changed, but there would always be need. You had to need—that was life, his father would say in that fat way of his. Need. It was all too far ahead. He had to wait and see.

"Can I help you?"

He turned to face the white smile of a bookseller. He'd just been standing there, the last guide returned to its place in the shelf. He'd just been standing there trying to come to terms with the limitations of his future. Nan, who made seven hundred and fifty thousand dollars a year, who owned three houses and two cars and tallied up several weeks of exotic vacations each quarter, whose only real limitation was her utter aloneness, had once told him that your thirties were about coming to terms with your limitations. So here he was. He smiled back at the bookseller.

"No thank you," he said clearly, spying his father pushing through the glass double doors. "No, I think I've got it all covered."

"Well," the bookseller said, "just let us know."

She owns this time. That's what they tell her. Own it, give in to it. Just rest, try to relax. No, the hands aren't going to help. We're just protecting you. Would you like some music? A sleep mask? Ginger ale? No, your kids aren't going to visit for a while. Your mother either. You need to rest. Everything else can wait.

"I want to go home," she said.

"A few days," the nurse said. "Then you'll be ready."

"I don't understand. I'm ready now."

"Hon. Look at me. Look at me. We need to see some consistent stability. And then you can go home."

"What about the kids?"

"Soon, Megan. Soon."

She was restless. You couldn't help but be restless. The phone didn't work. The television hurt. They said she was agitated and exhausted. Was the exhaustion making her agitated, or was it the other way around? They couldn't say. Sometimes she thought she heard her mother down the hall, arguing with them. They told her not to think about it. The incident with the epinephrine had cost her, and now she needed some time. A social worker visited. Own this time, she said, you deserve it. Megan had asked that the social worker not be allowed to see her again. A physical therapist came. She squeezed balls for a while. The physical therapist said he didn't need to come back. She couldn't read, she couldn't listen, she couldn't watch. It was all too tiring. She couldn't sleep because she was afraid—not of him, whoever he was, but of not waking up. She couldn't sleep, and she didn't want a sedative. Rest. Rest was lying in bed trying not to think. Once she heard the social worker in the hallway begging to see her. Or was it her mother. Or was it Warner and were there police and did she hear shouting? Or was it the children who crawled around like mice and got under the bed and were mice and crawled into bed and she couldn't stop flailing though she shouldn't she really shouldn't but they were mice and they flew around in muscular jolts inside her sheets. This is serious, she thought someone said. Maybe it wasn't so serious. Maybe it was a practical joke that she was playing on herself or Warner was playing on her or some greater entity was playing on both of them. Maybe her head hadn't been hurt. Maybe nothing had got to her. Oh yes it had. What was it? Repeat after me. I will relax. Relax.

"Would you like some water?"

She nodded. She reached for the cup but she had no hands to reach. They'd tied her wrists and ankles to the bed. She wasn't some puppet they could jerk around by the strings like this! When had this happened? How many days were they talking about now? Was it February? Was it March? Months were so big they were easy to track. Days were narrow, thin strips, tiny blocks on the page that you had to cram your handwriting into so you could schedule it all. Hours were. Minutes were. Seconds were. It was all impossible.

She couldn't quite track it back. The epinephrine had slipped and then she had slipped and then she'd crawled upward and then slipped again, crawled up and slipped.

Was that her mother in the hall?

"We're going to give you something mild, honey. We need to do another CAT scan. You can keep your eyes closed if you want. Just a little bit of a sedative, honey. To keep you still. Here it goes. It's going through the IV. You're going to relax, honey. There you go. Relax, now. Just relax."

It was the extent and degree and resilience of her confusion and agitation, they told Nan. They worried that perhaps the brain swelling was increasing despite the second operation.

"Could she die?" Nan asked, the question surprising her.

They shrugged. They didn't know. People with compound brain injuries can return to almost normal, they said. Let's just wait, they said. It was quite possible that Megan was the kind of person who got agitated, and that her agitation and confusion had less to do with the injury than they thought.

"She used to get migraines." Nan checked herself from clutching her hands. "For years she got them. I think she took something quite strong for them. Fiorinal. But then they stopped, once she got married."

Well, they said, we'll note that in her history. But let's just do the pictures.

"Okay," Nan said. "I hope they turn out great." She forced a laugh, and the two doctors in front of her dutifully smiled.

She sat in the waiting room outside the X-ray department when Megan was inside, as if that would help, and then she took her old seat outside the ICU. She tried to read the newspaper. *"I think he wanted more for his family," Richard Thrasher, Warner Lutz's boss over at MORE said. "I think he wanted more for us. It was why we hired him."* She snapped the newspaper closed.

Every few hours she would call to check on the children. Alan most often answered, although sometimes Sophie did. "Hello," she would say. "Is that you, Granny Nan?" They would chat about a show she had watched or a picture she had drawn, and then Nan would ask for Alan. They'd share updates—Daniel's last diaper, Megan's vital signs. She never talked to Warner.

"How's Ruth holding up?" she once asked.

"Oh, she's working." Alan sighed. "That's how she holds up. It distracts her. It's good." He caught his breath, as if talking were like running or swimming. "You know," he began, his voice lowered, "we've been thinking about school, about whether Sophie should go back."

"I don't think that's such a good idea."

"Okay." He breathed into the phone. "Why not?"

"What other kids might say. What seeing other moms would do to her. That kind of thing."

She could almost hear him shaking his head through the phone. "She needs to get back to school. She's almost five years old. Being around us isn't enough. She's ready."

"Can we talk about this later? I'm kind of preoccupied here."

"Okay," he said. "Okay."

"I have to run."

"It's been a whole week," he tried. "More."

She hung up without telling him to mind his own business. What did he know? And Ruth was so damn practical, so damn literal. You had to feel your way through this, there wasn't a decided path you could take. School in a week, summer day camp, chores, kindergarten in the fall—that wasn't how it worked. Frankly, she couldn't see Sophie going back to Allcomers. She couldn't see them staying in Charlotte. It was over for them in Charlotte. You didn't stick around where you'd been exposed, where your life had been opened up from the inside and revealed to be filled with anger, greed, and unrealized ambition. You left. You moved. You reemerged. That would be her strategy. She could see Megan and the kids back in Boston. Or in Atlanta. Warner? She couldn't see him anywhere.

"The pictures are good." Lyons was kneeling beside her, practically grinning through his instinctive reserve. "The edema is not as bad as I feared it might be. This thing should work itself out in a few days. So we'll see."

"What do you mean, 'good'?"

"It's a typical contracoup—the frontal lobe too has to heal, and it, too, looks better. We'll go easy on her. She's awake, groggy. Quiet. You could go see her, but we would like to keep her quiet for a while."

"Is she still"—Nan swallowed—"is she still tied down?"

"Just as a precaution."

"But when she wakes more fully and finds she's tied down, won't that make her situation more stressful?"

"It's a safety measure," he said with finality. He rose and folded his arms across his chest.

"What if I sat sort of out of view and didn't say a word. Could I take some of that responsibility?"

"Well." He looked at her. He really wasn't the jerk she'd thought; he was just another professional. "All right," he said. "I'll put in the order and we'll see how it goes. We do not want her hurting herself."

"Absolutely," she said.

. . .

At the turn into the parking lot her stomach clenched, but she just wanted to keep going, to keep going right on into the playground, to stand at the top of the red hill and shout as loudly as she could. Daddy drove right into handicapped parking even though he wasn't supposed to, and Pop-Pop got out and came around and opened her door for her and said, "Come on, tiger." She couldn't help giggling. No one had called her tiger before. Daniel kicked his feet in the car seat. Daddy cooed to him, and Pop-Pop took her hand and led her to the gate.

"Look who's back." Carol smiled so hard at her she looked as if her head would break. "We missed you, Sophie."

"Yes," she said proudly. "My daddy isn't in jail anymore and my mommy's almost all better. I've seen her twice."

"Good, good." She began to scoot her into the playground.

"I'm Sophie's grandfather." Pop-Pop shook Carol's hand seriously. "We'll be at home if anything comes up."

"I'm sure she'll be fine," Carol said.

Sophie raced to the picket fence to watch them leave. Simon was there. So was Jack. Elizabeth. Hannah. Dylan. She was the baddest of them all.

The car pulled back, and she felt something melt in her stomach. She tightened her belly.

"Fight the evil!" Dylan roared. And suddenly they all held pretend swords and they raced around the playground tromping on whoever got in the way, and the teachers let them because you were just supposed to work it out and she could keep up, she was running so fast, so free. If she hit the fence she'd practically burst through to the parking lot where the car wasn't anymore, but she couldn't think of that, she kept running and running to stay not far behind and not get tromped when they circled back. Her chest hurt from running so much, she was kicking the sand in her own face, but she kept going. She just wanted to tromp somebody, but there was nobody to tromp. Blow the whistle, she began to think. Just blow the whistle.

When Mary blew the whistle, she could have kissed it. She fell to the ground, choking, feeling how big the air was making her inside.

She walked with Hannah to the back of the line.

"Do you like my braids?" Hannah asked.

"They're all right." She wished Pop-Pop or somebody had done her hair, but nobody had, and she couldn't yet do it herself.

"We're getting Disney," Hannah said. "Do you want to come over?"

"Disney?" Now they were walking inside, into all that yellow that hurt her stomach. Up the steps to the Full Day Family room. "Wow," she said.

The classroom was calm. The Bad Guys were at the blocks. Hannah wasn't really a Bad Guy. Neither was she. The water table was set up in the middle. Paper and scissors and glue were lined up at the circle table.

"You want to glue?"

"Sure."

They cut and glued. Mary came. "Sweet Sophie," she said, and hugged her. She'd never called her that before. "How's your mom doing?"

"Good," Sophie said.

"And your little brother?"

"Good."

"Well, if there's anyone you want to talk to, I'm here, sweetie."

"Okay." Sophie nodded her head.

"Good work with the scissors. You must be practicing."

They watched Mary walk to the next station.

"I have such a headache," Sophie said.

"Could you pass the glue?" Hannah asked.

And then she did want to talk. She didn't quite know why, she didn't exactly know what it meant, to go and just talk, just speak maybe to hear your voice and see what it said. She saw Mary standing in the corner smiling at her, and she put down her scissors and walked right up to Mary.

"Mary," she said. "I'm ready to talk."

"Okay," Mary said slowly, drawing out the "a" until it seemed to end on its own. "Should we go to the Quiet Corner?"

Sophie shook her head. She didn't like the Quiet Corner. It was behind a strung-up bedsheet that kept you in like the curtain around the potty in the bathroom. "Outside?" she suggested.

"Hmm," Mary hummed. She was just so big Sophie wanted to hug her to see if she could hold all that. "Carol, Sophie and I are going outside for a minute. Okay?"

Carol glanced up from the water table. Sophie saw her eyes thinking. "Okay."

It was all okay. Mary took her hand, and they walked out of the classroom, down the hall, down the stairs, and out the blue door to the playground. Mary looked at her watch.

"We can only stay for a few minutes," she said. "Threes and fours get the playground soon."

Sophie sat high on the steps to the tree house. Mary stood beside her. They were almost shoulder to shoulder. Mary's eyes were nearly green, sometimes blue. Her glasses were thick.

"So," Mary said. "What have you been doing all week?"

"Shopping." Sophie hugged her knees. It wasn't too cold. "Playing with Daniel. Watching television. The playground when it's sunny. Candyland. Eating pizza. My Granny Nan's with us whenever Pop-Pop and Daddy aren't. She spends the night and they stay in a hotel. She double locks the door and chain locks it and leaves the kitchen light on all night. She sleeps with the phone right under her bed. My Granny Nan says it's temporary. When Mommy comes home it'll be different."

"What do you think about that?" Mary said.

"I'm ready for Mommy to come home."

"I bet."

"I miss my mommy," Sophie said. She missed the way she smelled and how soft her voice was, even when she got mad. She missed running her fingers through her hair and hiding her face in there. She missed climbing into bed with her in the earliest part of the morning and making her watch television with her. Now her hair was all pointy and short, and her face seemed hard and white. She felt her lips quiver, and suddenly she didn't want to talk anymore. She felt sleepy inside. The blue door opened and out marched the threes and fours, their faces shiny.

"I guess we'd better go," Mary said.

Sophie stood and dusted herself. "I think it was long enough."

"Good," Mary said. "I'm glad."

. . .

"Warner?"

Someone was tugging at him, somewhere at his foot. He turned away from it, but it held him fast by his big toe. He grinned into the familiar pillow of his familiar bed.

"Dad?" he mumbled. It was the way he'd always woken him in the mornings. Just came on in and wagged his big toe. It was so gentle. He tried to open his eyes.

"I think somebody wants you."

Warner's eyes opened. He could hear Daniel squalling. They'd all been napping. He loved that Nan was at the hospital most of the day. He loved that Sophie was back at preschool. He loved that it was just the three of them in the town house.

"Okay." He smiled and pushed himself from bed, knuckled the sleep from his eyes, ascended the stairs.

Daniel was standing in the crib. He stopped crying as soon as he saw him.

"That's my boy," Warner heard himself say, picking him up, and held him to his chest, feeling the absurdly rapid banging of his little heart. "How's my boy? Are you Daddy's boy? How's my boy?" Daniel held on as Warner carried him downstairs, the short arms not quite reaching around his back, the head melted into his shoulder, pillowed heavily against the side of his neck as if still asleep. "Rice cereal?" Warner said.

"Um-hum," Daniel said.

Warner's father was already on the phone. "Right," he kept saying. "Right, I know. We just thought it was time." He looked sadly at Daniel's sleepiness and shrugged. "I know. Yes, I know." He listened while Daniel and Warner got out the blue measuring cup and orange box and began to make rice cereal. "Okay. Yes." He hung up.

"Nan?" Warner said, not looking up.

"She wasn't too happy about Sophie." He lifted Daniel from the floor and took him to the high chair. Warner followed with the bowl. Daniel sat placidly as he was clicked in, and started immediately in on his food.

"Anything else?" Warner asked. "About Megan."

"Didn't say a word."

After the baby ate Warner changed him and they snapped him in the stroller. Outside the day was bright blue, boldly sunny. They walked slowly. Perennials bloomed from their pine needle beds, crape myrtles poked tiny tight buds into the warming air. The sun glared off the redbrick facades of the cloisters of apartments and town houses. Cars glided over freshly laid asphalt. Beyond a fence swirled the clink and quiet talk of maintenance workers inspecting the clubhouse pool. The drive dipped and curved toward the green playground. It was nearly February.

"So what are you going to do?" his father said.

He wanted to say something, but his throat was empty. How there was so much sameness and sterility in their life but how overwhelmingly serene it all could have been. How it had broken. How he had broken it. Gently he pulled Daniel from the stroller and set him in the swing and pushed.

"Have you thought about where you're going to live?"

"No." He could have lied and said yes and lied some more, but he couldn't.

"It's draining," his father said.

"Sure is." He stopped in midpush. It struck him that that was the way he used to describe the kids. Now he saw them as sweet infusions, jolts of hope and sensory pleasure.

Daniel looked back, his face expectant. Warner helped him swing, and he giggled.

"You'll need money." His father sounded almost helpless; he didn't have it.

"Don't worry about me." Now he was tickling the boy's chubby calves each time he swung back. How he wished he could just always see his face.

"I'm going to have to go up soon."

Warner nodded.

"I mean, what will you do? How will you get to see the kids?"

He kept his eye on the swing, on Daniel's round head with the ears sticking out, on the doughy forearms and the dimples of elbows that wrapped tightly around the edge of the bucket seat. He whimpered; he'd had enough. Warner caught the swing and lifted him out and held him to him, the soft face, the nose rumpling against his chest, the shallow exhalations damp against his shirt. The sleepy cereal smell of him. What a boy, he kept thinking. What a boy, what a boy, what a boy.

"Warner?" his dad said.

He couldn't say anything.

There was a sound that was like a bell that wasn't a bell. Her mother sat by the bed watching, her face anxious and judgmental. Megan couldn't help thinking about that stupid sports metaphor that Warner liked to use, about staying within yourself, not overswinging, just connecting and making contact. Did he really talk like that? What *was* he talking about? There wasn't any sound. She'd just have to stay within herself, not say too much, just to get home. She just wanted to get home. Hospitals. She looked at her unleashed arms. She wasn't crazy. Just stay within yourself.

"How you feeling?" her mother asked. She would ask that. She couldn't ever not ask. What were they talking about?

"I'm fine, thanks."

"That's great, honey." The overreaction, the overvaluation. Couldn't she ever just not say or ask anything? Couldn't she ever just keep it to herself?

"I think I'll sleep," Megan said.

"That's good, honey."

She shut her eyes and waited for her mother to leave. She wouldn't. Why couldn't she be more likable? Why couldn't anybody be more likable? She'd leave. She had to leave *sometime*.

"You know what you could do for me?" she said, forcing herself to open her eyes and look at her mother's eager face. "It's nearly spring, isn't it? Maybe you could take Sophie clothes shopping. She'd love that. Maybe you could take her now?"

"Well, actually"—there went one hand into the other. God, everything was horrid—"I have to stay." She practically blushed. "I made a deal with your doctor. I stay, and he keeps you out of restraints."

"Oh." Oh it *was* horrid. She was horrid. They were all horrid. "I see. Thank you."

"Anything for you, sweetie." Her mother was blushing. If Megan could have hit her, she would have. She would.

"Thank you," she said again, staying within herself. She pushed up in bed. "I guess I could eat something."

"Oh. Okay." She gathered the call handle and rang it

before Megan could do anything. "What do you think you could eat?"

"Anything," she said blandly. She knew she had to show she could eat. "Whatever they want me to, I guess."

"There's nothing wrong with your stomach," her mother said, again clasping her hands. "I think it's whatever you want that they have."

"Chicken?" Megan guessed. "Or pasta."

"That sounds good," her mother tried to joke. "I wouldn't mind having some of that."

The nurse came. The food came. She walked the few feet to the bathroom. She peed. She ate. Her mother sat there with her hands tightly together. She could hardly bear it. She ate some more. They talked about the food. Her mother timidly intimated she was hungry. Megan offered her a chocolate milkshake she couldn't stomach. Her mother gulped it down.

"This is really quite good," she said. She finished it loudly. Megan tried not to cringe.

"You know what I think I'd love," her mother said, "I'd love a hamburger." She was being cheerful. God she meant well. Megan smiled and finished the chicken, finished the linguine. The nurse came and congratulated her. Was the day almost over? It ought to be over.

"I'll sit with her for a while," the nurse offered.

"Actually," Megan said. "I thought I would sleep."

"I'll still sit with you," the nurse said.

Her mother kissed her on the cheek. "Back soon," she said. She swished from the room.

Why was she so damn ungenerous? She smiled at the nurse, trying to look grateful, and shut her eyes. She couldn't find the click, the click inside that made her ungenerous, the click inside that had made her a little crazy. The door she had gone through, or whatever it was. The hole that had opened. She could feel her hands clutching into fists. Stop that, she thought. Stop that, she said.

"Stop what?" the nurse asked.

"Oh," she murmured. "Oh, I'm just dreaming."

"That was quick," the nurse said.

"Just tired," she said.

Where was the hole? Where was the door? Where was it black? A head injury. It was up in the head. It wasn't in her chest, which hurt nonetheless. It wasn't her heart. It wasn't her soul. It was her head. She just had to get out of her head. She couldn't spend her time looking for that hole or that door or that click. She wouldn't find the answer to anything. You didn't find it: you either got over what had happened or gave in to it. She had kids. She had Warner. She needed to get out of her head.

"Megan?"

She nodded.

"Do you think it would help if I secured your wrists again?"

She nodded sadly. It was such a long way back from where she had been the last days to where she had always used to be.

"You've been hospitalized before, haven't you?"

She let her head nod.

"You don't look like someone who used to be hospitalized."

She had to smile at that.

"Depression?"

Was it ever anything else?

"You were . . . a teenager?"

Wasn't everybody?

"How long?"

She didn't want to say.

"You know what I think?" the woman asked, tying her second wrist. "I think if we could get some history here, maybe we could get some answers."

It was five weeks. It was on and off medications. It was nothing, really. No history. She hadn't taken anything since. Hadn't had a migraine in ten years.

"The brain is very complicated," the nurse said.

When she woke, her mother sat by the bed reading an Anne Tyler novel and sipping grapefruit juice. The nurse was gone. Her wrists weren't tied. She could have imagined some of it. She could have imagined all of it.

"How you feeling?" her mother said softly.

"Okay." She thought about it. Her head felt unreasonably clear, as if she could see in there. "Much better, I think."

"Let's hope that was the last dip," her mother said.

"Yes," she said.

Her mother kept reading. Her back was rigid, and she set the grapefruit juice on the floor and tentatively massaged one hand with the other. She looked as if her feelings had been hurt.

"Did the nurse talk to you?" Megan asked.

She nodded.

"I just want to get out of here."

"I'm working on it," she said. She didn't look up from her book.

Megan sighed. "It was almost twenty years ago."

"Sixteen."

"Whatever."

"It's not relevant," her mother said.

"Of course it isn't."

"You sound so much clearer today."

"I'm ready." She smiled as naturally as she could.

"Good."

She maneuvered to the side of the bed, made sure the back of her gown was closed, and stepped to the bathroom. Inside, she shut the door. She was alone. No one could see her. How odd not to be seen. What did they see when they looked at her? The only child of parents who had divorced more than twenty years ago and still hated each other? A feeble suicide attempt at nineteen and a half? A battered woman at thirty-five? What did they see? Where was grace when she needed it, where was mercy, where was serenity? If only she could be serene. If only she hadn't gotten hurt like this. Struck. How did she know? Was it something they'd said? No, it was something she knew, something she'd seen. The hammer on the table within reach. The nails on the floor. That hammer. The door gong going. A voice, her voice. What did it sound like? Hello, she said.

"What?" her mother said, out there through the wood and plaster.

"Nothing," Megan said. She ran the tap while she heard herself muttering. Nothing, nothing, nothing. She looked at the water coming out of the faucet. She could splash it on her face, as if that would help her. She wasn't a victim. She didn't need help. You made your own destiny. So they were middle class; that didn't mean they were mediocre. How could they have ever thought that? Well, you thought what you thought. That couldn't be helped. But what you did, how you did it—beautiful children, art, service, sensibility, morality. They'd never cheated, they tried just to do well. God, he was always trying. Somehow, they had failed. Their dream hadn't really ever been money so much as it had been comfort, occasional luxury, adventure. Fairly common desires, when you thought about it that way, and she did want to think about it that way and wanted him to think about it too. So they couldn't get the new car, the big house. But there was much they could have had. Was it really over? Were they over? Was it over for the children?

"Are you okay?" her mother called.

"Yes," she said, so easily it stunned her. She was finding her way through, or feeling as if she were, or finding out that she *was* through. She shut off the water and opened the door.

Home

W hat has it taught you?"

"What has it taught me," she repeated, trying to be patient.

"Yes." He crossed his legs, pushed his glasses up his nose. "Any experience can teach you things . . . or so they say. What has it taught you?"

He was the fifth or sixth her mother had made her see or the assistant D.A. had made her see or both of them had made her see. He was the last one. It didn't matter what her mother told her the paper said or the radio said. A woman who was beaten, a woman who had some sense beaten into her, a woman who . . . He was the last one. She barely listened to herself speak as she watched him while he wrote on his pad. She was going along to get along.

It wasn't denial. It wasn't mercy. It wasn't surrender. She was the one who had woken up. She was the one who could live. She was the one who had to go forward. If you took it away, then what was there? If you removed it from the equation, if you recommenced as if it had never happened, then what? What were they? What had they been? What was he? What was she? Who were they? If you couldn't know, if you'd never have access to knowing, then you had to look at everything else. Those twelve years without the past two weeks. All that time. The children. The places they'd lived. The good vacations, the bad vacations, the good jobs, the bad jobs, the jobs that didn't matter, the negativism, the optimism, each other's families, the bad dates, the good dates, the disagreements, the fights, the hate, the love, the sex, the making out, the making love, dinners, lunches, breakfasts, midnights, sleepless nights, birthdays, holidays, every day.

If he said he was sorry, she might know. If he couldn't look at her, or if he looked at her a certain way, or if he just looked a certain way or sounded a certain way or kissed or touched a certain way, she could maybe know. But if she couldn't tell, she just couldn't tell. If she let it eat her up, or if she just left him, then her life seemed impossible, as if it wasn't she who was living it but somebody else, somebody who was giving in to what had happened. She didn't want to give in, she just wanted to get past it. Sometimes she found herself wishing, if only she were still asleep, if only she had just been killed, if only she had turned. She could have seen, or she could have never known that anything had happened.

The ripe red travel bag her mother had bought for the occasion sat beside her chair, stuffed with a nightgown, a pajama set, two bathrobes, a bath towel, a washcloth, a hand towel, slippers, and a makeup kit. Her mother had mail-ordered from Neiman Marcus and Nordstrom and found one thing at Victoria's Secret in SouthPark. It was all oranges, reds, bright, warm, imported. Part floral. All natural fiber. Practically a trousseau.

• • •

She could not see how it could work. "So you're saying," she said again, "that *he'll* stay down here while you stay upstairs in Daniel's room."

"Right," Megan said. She still had her sunglasses on, in the dark, narrow town house, and to Nan she couldn't help but look a little eccentric, a little deranged.

"I just don't see it," she said over the background noise of the television. Thank god for the television. It was sometimes the only way you could have a conversation with the kids around.

"I'll be all right. Look, I've thought it out, believe it or not, and it's the only fair thing to do."

Nan waved her hands. "After what he did? The only fair thing is a good long prison term. Or something pharmaceutical. Or both. But not this. I really can't allow this, sweetie."

"Can't allow it, Mom? Can't allow it?" She appeared almost to be smiling. "I passed all the tests. I was released—"

"Shhh," Sophie yelled from the couch.

"Look." Megan dropped her voice. "You can stay too, if that would make you feel better. We can pull out the extra mattress from storage and you can sleep on Sophie's floor."

"On my floor!" Sophie squealed delightedly. "Oh, Granny Nan!"

"Megan." She slumped in a chair by the dining table. It cracked and nearly gave out; everything in this place was either almost broken or cheap. The girl needed new furniture, a new house, a new life. "I don't really want to have to do that."

"You could stay at a hotel."

"Well, actually," she said, feeling her hands moving into

each other. "Actually I was thinking you all could come to Atlanta."

"Atlanta?" Her daughter stared at her. "What would we do in Atlanta? Sophie has school. I still have a job."

"I have plenty of room."

She finally took off her sunglasses. She squinted and studied the carpet.

"Just for a couple of weeks," Nan said.

"I don't think so. Look, Warner's due over in a few hours. I'd like to clean up and get my act together. You can watch the kids or not. But he is coming—and I did tell him he could stay. It's his place, too."

"I don't believe this."

"Stop making it about what you believe." She shook her head sadly and looked directly at her.

"I know, sweetie. It's just—"

"Forget it, Mom. Okay?" She headed upstairs with her red travel bag.

So what *was* she supposed to do? The children sat side by side on the couch, television-glazed. She ought to get them out of here, but then that would leave Megan alone with him, and she couldn't abide that. Maybe she could just run the kids to the mall for an hour, be back in time. She picked up their portable and dialed Sandy. She liked to call at least four times a day. Sandy wasn't in. "Well, give me someone to talk to who knows something," she told the receptionist. It wasn't quite ten, but they all ought to be there.

"Nan?" It was Del. "Sandy's out sick today."

"Oh."

"Not to worry. We've got everything under control." He gave a brief rundown on the day ahead. Nothing terribly important. He would send her a few faxes. "Human Resources called," he finished. "They wondered if they should make your leave indefinite."

"No, no, no." She felt her heart pinch. "What's today?"

"Tuesday," he said quietly.

"I'll be in by Thursday. I'll call them directly."

"I wasn't going to call anybody without your say-so."

"I'll speak to you soon," she said.

Work. How could she let it slip like this? She called the airline and got a seat on the seven a.m. Thursday flight, then clicked off the television.

"Children," she said, "we're going to the mall!"

Daniel murmured, and Sophie jumped up and down. Nan felt his diaper, gathered the changing bag and the baby, and took hold of Sophie's hand.

"We're going to the mall," she called up the dark stairs. "We'll be back in less than an hour."

"Okay!"

At the mall they threw pennies in the fountain, and she let them each pick one thing from the educational toy store. She kept checking her watch. It was better to be home with the children than not there at all. She steered them back to the car. Daniel was screaming, and Sophie kept saying she wanted to go to just one more store. She buckled them wriggling into their seats. Sometimes it was such a wrestle with them she couldn't quite see how Megan would manage. She pulled left from the lot and knew that she had to turn right soon. Daniel wailed.

"Could you see what's wrong with your brother?" she asked Sophie while trying to find the next street.

"He's crying," Sophie said.

"I know that," she said, changing lanes, thinking was this her right turn, or was it the next light. "Why?"

"I don't know," Sophie said. "I think he wants to go back to the mall."

"Uh-hunh." It was her turn. She was sure of it. She took it and raced down a double lane bordered by a high brick wall to either side, beyond which protruded colossal brick and porticoed houses in the latest neo-Federalist style. She was nouveau riche, but she wasn't that nouveau riche. She felt fairly certain she'd made the wrong turn, and she wanted to ask Sophie if she had, but she kept driving. The walls clung to the road, opened briefly for guardhouses to either side. She couldn't turn. A red light flamed at the end. That was their road. She took a left.

"This is Fairview," Sophie said.

"Yes, I know, honey."

"I think Daniel's asleep."

"Thank goodness."

"We'll be home soon."

"Yes we will." It was the right road. She couldn't help but feel thrilled. They passed a familiar strip mall and drove uphill to a traffic light. She knew it wasn't their turn. You should be able to see Crape Myrtle Hill from Fairview. Beyond a private school sunk in a valley of freshly planted sod was a second light. Not here either. Probably still a bit to go. She sailed through a third and then a fourth light.

"Granny Nan," Sophie whimpered. "Granny Nan, you missed our turn."

"I did?" She braked, and someone's horn blared behind her. She had to keep going.

"We're getting lost," Sophie cried. "I want to go home."

"We'll just take the next turn," Nan said. "Not a problem." Anxiously she eyed Daniel in the rearview. Beyond the divider, the side gate of Crape Myrtle Hill whizzed by.

"*Is* there a next turn?" Sophie wailed.

A piercing shriek startled her. Daniel was awake.

"We're almost there," she told them.

Beside her the divider wouldn't quit: you couldn't make a left turn to save your life, it seemed. She needed a stoplight. Where were all the intersections?

"We're going farther away," Sophie said tearfully.

How could there not be any intersections? Wasn't that odd? She touched the open collar of her blouse and found she had broken into a sweat. Come on, come on. Give her a left. Was it too much to ask for a left in this town? A huge Baptist church rambled by. They ought to have had a left into that. Hypocrites. She couldn't buy a left. Daniel was absolutely shrieking, and she couldn't turn to check on him because she had to keep hunting for a turn. She could make a right but it all looked so labyrinthine and subdivided back there, and none of it was in a direction she needed to go.

A light up ahead. She hit her blinker. It was already on, ticking metronomically. Now they'd been gone over an hour. "We're going home," she said as she swung them through the intersection in a frantic U-turn. She revved the engine, and they soared back down the way they'd come.

"Granny Nan," Sophie shrilled, "you tipped my seat."

She glanced in the rearview. Sophie's seat was upright, no harm done. Beyond her head whirled flashing blue lights. Unbelievable.

"I guess it's not my day," she said as she pulled to the side.

"Whaddya mean?" Sophie asked.

"You'll see."

She dug in the glove compartment for the rental agreement and rolled down the automatic window.

"I guess it was an illegal U-turn?" she said.

"Yes, ma'am." The officer took her driver's license and registration. "Atlanta, Georgia?" she said.

"Yes, Officer."

"Those," she nodded to the backseat, "I expect are your grandchildren."

For once they were quiet. "Yes, Officer."

"Well, a U-turn when it says no U-turn is illegal in all fifty states, but I think we can give you a warning this time. Let me call it in and I'll let you know." She marched back to her car.

"Maybe it is my day," Nan said to the rearview mirror. She almost felt like giggling. Of course they were late. She pulled out her cell phone and called.

"Hello," Megan answered on the first ring.

"Is he there?"

"Not yet, Mom. The kids all right?"

"Of course. See you soon." She started to put the phone back into her bag.

"Eh," Daniel said. "Eh. Eh."

"He wants your phone," Sophie said.

"Eh, eh."

"Well, he can't have it," Nan said. "I'm sorry, sweetie." She smiled sympathetically at Daniel.

"Eh, eh, eh," he began to yowl. "EH. EH." His face was turning red and his nose squinched up as he shut his eyes and frantically cried. "EH EH. EH. EHHHH." He was practically purple.

Sophie held her ears. She was laughing. "Can't you give him the phone," she shouted.

"Well." What could be the harm. In the rearview mirror the officer was returning, and Daniel kept screaming, nearing blue. "Okay. Okay." She handed him the phone.

"Here you go, ma'am." The officer offered the documents. "You're all set."

"Thank you," she said.

She rolled up her window and restarted the car. Daniel cooed at the phone. Sophie stayed quiet. "Here we go," she said.

They were nearly home when she heard a sound like the snapping of a branch underfoot. Her head jerked, but she was determined not to miss her turn.

"What was that?" she asked, although she knew.

Daniel was gurgling gleefully, almost in a trill.

"Did he break the phone?"

"He didn't mean to," Sophie said.

She sighed. "I know."

When they parked, she saw the phone in two pieces in his lap. Before she could stop herself, she slammed her hand against the dashboard. Sophie jumped.

"Damn it," Nan heard herself say anyway. "I needed that phone." She shoved the car door open, her arms trembling. She got Sophie out of her seat and scooted her to the sidewalk, went around and opened Daniel's door. He'd broken off the entire hinged mouthpiece. Narrow shreds of yellow wiring gave out from the receiver, as if he'd bitten the phone in two. She yanked it from him and stuffed it into her handbag. Quickly she unpinched the Y-shaped plastic seat guard and wrenched it over his face, clipping his nose. She twisted him from the seat and stood him on the asphalt. Her face was burning. *Okay*, she muttered. *Okay, okay, okay.* "Go on," she tried to say cheerfully. "Go on over to your sister." Bawling, he staggered against her instead, clasped his arms around her knees, and cried wetly into her silk pants. She took a deep breath. It was just a goddamn phone, damn it. It wasn't anything. She willed herself to pick him up. He sobbed into her shoulder.

Megan came out of the town house, practically at a run.

"What's the matter?" she said, reaching for the baby. "I could hear him all the way inside."

"Nothing," Nan said. "Nothing at all." She held the baby from Megan and headed for the door. "He just broke my cell phone and it made him a little bit upset."

"I'll take him," Megan insisted.

"Please." She was in the stifling town house now. "I can handle it. I want to."

Daniel bawled against her shoulder. She headed upstairs with him, into the tiny closed peace of his bedroom. Their study. Soon to be Megan's room. Whatever they were calling it this week. She shut the door and let him cry, standing in that awful little room with the one window and the big desk and the crib and the foldout futon sofa, with the open bathroom door gaping at her with its green and silver wallpapered mouth. What a place, she kept thinking. What a place, what a place, what a place. She couldn't wait to leave.

He came at four, right when he'd said he would. In the morning newspaper there'd been an article about two families who continued living five houses away on the same street in Raleigh, despite the fact that one family's son had been convicted of murdering the other family's daughter. No good parallels there, no redemption for anyone. Then Polly Edwards had called and told Warner without enthusiasm that the charges probably would be dropped: there were no witnesses and no forensic evidence. He sat in the car outside of the town house, looking at Nan's rental car, taking in the solid redbrick wall of their home. His bag was in the trunk, hidden, as if he hadn't had to take anything with him, as if he'd never been exiled. It was his home, too, Megan had told him on the phone, without any tinge to her voice, and he wondered if somehow the accident had soldered off her emotional connections, blunted her.

He got out, bumping past Nan's car, revulsion in his throat. She really shouldn't be here. It was just between the two of them. He was already flushed when he knocked on the door—you didn't want to use your key in this kind of situation. He hoped the children were home.

"Hey."

She'd swung the door open so quickly he knew he had that frozen-in-the-headlights look.

"Hi." He began to lean forward to kiss her, not quite taking her in, but then he held himself back. She didn't move.

"Where're your bags? I told you—"

"They're in the car." He nodded sideways.

"Don't you think you should get them?"

"Your mom here?"

She sighed, a whisper of irritation that he easily remembered. "Upstairs with the kids."

"I wanted to ask, but I didn't think it was right."

"That never stopped you before," she said, without humor, but without rancor either.

Her face was pale, with the same nearly unlined sweetness. He winced at her bristly hair. "You don't look any different," he said.

"Why should I?" She opened the door wider to let him in. "It was all in the back of my head."

He gave a little shiver as he stepped across the threshold and walked past her, as if maybe she'd decide at the last instant to clobber him a few times. You could feel guilty no matter what the truth was. You could deny a truth no matter how guilty you were.

The ground floor was as chaotic and beige as he remembered it. Since his father had left five days ago, he hadn't been inside, hadn't seen the kids. There was the square of kitchen in its yellow-and-green-plaid wallpaper, there was the too-low pass-through, there was the dining table, the coffee table, the stained couch, the queen bed, the television perched beside the French doors that opened to the patch of a patio and the storage closet. A green dinosaur rocker, a red trike, and a blue high chair rose out of the beige carpet and blond wood and oatmeal patterns of the long living-dining-bed room.

"So?" she said. Her arms were folded against her chest. She'd lost weight. Her cheeks had greater definition, slight color.

"So."

"How are you?"

"How are *you*?"

"Not too bad." She went into the kitchen, and he followed her. She ran a glass of water from the tap. "There isn't anything wrong with me."

"That's good."

She sipped the water and stared at him. "Don't you want to see the kids?" she said suddenly.

He blushed. It was the old argument that he never had the natural instinct to rush up to check on the kids whenever he came in late from work or a business trip. "Of course," he said.

"Then again," she sighed, a slight smirk, "my mother's up there."

Was it all going to be a test? Maybe so. He grinned. "I'll go right on up."

Up the stairs he decided she was herself, but strange, more ironic, distant, more substantial. Was he himself? He couldn't tell. He was flustered, mumbling. Like a first date. The hierarchy was all wrong. He had everything at stake and she could deny him and there would be nothing he could do. Just stay within yourself, he coached. Whoever the fuck that was. Don't let yourself get away. Don't be yourself. Or be yourself. Or just chuck it and run. Or have a seat on the stairs and think this thing through just a little more carefully. Those kids—they giggled through Sophie's shut bedroom door. He could stand outside it and not knock and after a few minutes go on downstairs and report that everything was okay. Was he such a coward? He was at the top of the stairs. Four steps and he was at the door. Did he even need to knock? What if one of them was tight against the door, and he opened it and sent somebody headfirst into the hard corner of the bookcase? Gently he opened the door.

"Daddy!" Sophie raced toward him.

"Dada!" Daniel raised his arms and gave a little hop.

They were at his legs, holding him. He couldn't look up. He held them to him, waiting, mourning the time he'd lost. Daniel slobbered happily against his neck. Nan had surrendered the room.

"So how have you been?" he asked.

"Great!" Sophie said.

"Doo," Daniel said.

"Good?" he asked.

"Doo," the baby affirmed.

"I wish Granny Nan weren't leaving," Sophie said.

"That *is* too bad." He tried to swallow his elation. "I'm sure she'll be back soon."

"That's what she said. Or maybe we'll visit her first."

"Maybe."

"Mommy's back forever."

"I know."

Sophie stood on one foot. "Do I have to go to school tomorrow?"

"Dada," Daniel said, as if he couldn't quite believe it.

"Yes," he said. "School it is."

"Can we play Candyland?"

He looked doubtfully at Daniel. He always swatted the pieces across the board and threw the cards everywhere. "Sure," Warner said.

"Great!" Sophie ran for the game, ran toppling back with it.

"Ha da!" Daniel shouted.

"We can try." Warner shrugged at Sophie. They both laughed as they sat cross-legged on the floor. They set up the pieces and for the moment Daniel let them play.

"So what have you guys been up to?"

"Shopping." Sophie grinned. "Visiting Mommy at the hospital. Shopping some more."

Daniel came over and sat in his lap. He felt absurdly happy. "You get good stuff?"

"Oh yeah."

His gingerbread man fell behind while hers marched resolutely toward the kingdom. Daniel pinched dully at his wrist. Warner hoped for a quick finish. He picked Plumpy.

"Oh Daddy!"

He moved his piece all the way back. The games with their trapdoors. If only he could keep falling through, then she would have to win. Daniel rose and stepped toward the board.

"Whee." Warner swung him back.

He kicked the air. "Ha da!" he said. "Ha da!"

"Hurry," Warner said to Sophie, as her hand hovered over which card to pick.

"I'm hurrying," she said.

"Ha da!" the baby squealed and squirmed. In an instant he was free. Cards flew. The two pieces scattered.

"Daddy!" Sophie shrieked.

"Well, we tried." Warner gathered the cards.

"That's not good enough," she said. "We have to start over."

"Maybe when he naps."

"He *already* napped."

"Oh."

Daniel finished kicking around and stood squawking at them.

"Send him down to Mommy," Sophie said.

"I'm right here." Megan stood in the door, her face indifferent. He couldn't tell how long she'd been there. "We need to talk about dinner."

"Right," he said. He rose to his feet. Again his face was red.

"We were *playing*," Sophie insisted.

It was all so intricate and repetitious, you could cut it a hundred different ways and still never defuse it.

"How about some television," he said, although he knew it was against the rules. "You guys want to watch TV?"

"Nickelodeon," Sophie roared.

"Weewee," Daniel said. He turned to Warner and held up his arms. "Weewee."

He scooped him up. Megan touched him quickly. "I'll be right down." She escaped into the bathroom.

"Did I ever tell you I saw you once on TV?" Sophie held his free hand as they navigated the stairs. "I don't think I told you. It was when you were in jail."

"I was never really in jail," he said.

"At the police," she corrected herself. "I saw a picture of you on TV. Grandma wouldn't let me watch it."

"Hmm." He was wondering how much of this Nan was overhearing from wherever she was lingering in the town house.

"Are you famous, Daddy?" She jumped the last step.

"No," he said in a low voice. He set Daniel on the floor and hunted for the clicker.

"I didn't think so," Sophie said. "Otherwise we'd be rich and we're not rich, are we, Daddy?"

"No," he said quietly. "We're not." He flinched when he turned on the television, half expecting to see himself.

"So you were on television, too." Nan came out from the kitchen, drying a cast-iron frying pan that was already dry. The kids sat again on the sofa. "You really shouldn't be here."

He looked at her holding the frying pan so tightly. How odd it was to think that in all the years they'd known each other they'd never spoken a contrary word. And now this. Nan had been good at pushing him aside whenever she wanted to spend time with Megan or the kids, and he'd been good to her face about letting himself be pushed aside. They'd both fiercely levered Megan, weighing on her whenever either of them got her alone. He was sick of Nan, just sick of her. He looked at her.

"So you're not staying," he said.

"I used to think you were different," she said, as they brushed against each other into the kitchen. "That you at least made an effort to understand. But you're just inadequate."

"What do you want me to say?" He swallowed, trying to shut himself up. "You're just someone older and alone who takes too good care of herself and will outlive everybody she knows. You've reached an age where all you want to do is satisfy yourself and beyond that you regard everyone else's task as being in service of you. You do this thing with your hands like you're flexing at some bodybuilder contest—"

She swung the pan so quickly and so hard that it seemed to be through him before he was aware that it had even moved. It was her goddamn tennis that did it. A kind of squeal escaped him, and he choked it back. He was sitting on the floor.

"What the hell's going on here?"

It was Megan, innocent Megan.

"Nothing," her mother said quickly. "It was nothing. Not really."

He couldn't yet talk. He was sitting in something wet, and to his embarrassment he knew what it was.

"Jesus," Megan said.

He moved his mouth, but no word came. That was a relief, he knew. She'd connected right below the rib cage, had met only flesh and crushed through to an organ or two. What was there? Stomach. Intestines. Maybe a pancreas. A liver. His liquor-basted liver. Ohhh. He groaned, and it came out thin and piercing. Of course no one was asking if he was all right. Still he couldn't get up. He felt soaked. He was soaked.

"I really have to go," Nan said. "This isn't satisfactory for me at all, and I'm not going to stay to watch it happen." She handed the frying pan to Megan and picked up the phone. "I need to change my reservation." She walked with it into the living room.

Ahhh, Warner thought he said. He could hear Megan counting to ten in slower and slower repetitions.

"I'm not supposed to be dealing with stress," she muttered.

Then she shouldn't have taken him in, he thought. He shouldn't have let her. He should have waited.

"You can't go telling my mother everything I think about her," she murmured. "She's *my* mother for Christ's sake."

"Right," he managed.

"Are you going to be able to clean yourself up?" She tapped a toe by his puddle.

"Uh-hunh," he said.

"That's a yes?"

He nodded.

"That's good. Could you do it soon? I don't want the kids to see this." From the living room they could hear her mother talking to the children in an anxious, unusual voice. "I'd better go out there." She stuck the frying pan in the sink. "Get yourself together, okay?"

On the sofa her mother had glued herself between the two children and she was talking while tears ran down her cheeks and Sophie was crying too though it was clear she was also trying to watch the television. Daniel babbled against all the words. As far as Megan could tell her mother was mourning having to leave the children behind.

"I tried, oh I tried," she was saying. "I'm so sorry, you guys. My cuties. I'll see you as soon as I can."

"Mom," she said. "Mom, please. If you have to leave, you have to leave. But let's not—"

"This is so awful." She tried to wipe the tears off her face, but they kept coming. "So awful I can't believe it's happening."

"What's happening? Whatever has happened has happened. It's over."

"Oh god. My two sweeties." She hugged them again to her, then pushed herself from the couch. "I just can't believe all this. You." She was looking at Megan now. "You really shouldn't be doing this. I've tried. I'll be back. But this is something terrible. I just know it."

"Are we so certain it's him, Mom?" Her voice was trembling. Now she just wanted her to leave. "Are we just so certain? It's Warner, Mom. I know Warner."

"Did you know I was going to hit him with the frying pan? Did you know he was going to hit you with that hammer? Do you have any idea what an absolute asshole your father was? *Nobody,*" her mom glared at her furiously, "*knows anybody.*"

When she had finally left it felt to Megan as if nothing had gone unsaid, that all the air in the town house was filled with words, that there was no air. She just wanted some things unspoken again. What a relief it would be, not to hear, not to know, just to think, as if to have it all said meant that there was nothing left to think, that you couldn't think, there was no thought if there was none of it unsaid. The town house was still crowded without her, but god the air was coming back in, even if it was heavy.

For so long, she felt, she'd just been going along, recovering, trying to recover, not trying to think or say or do anything, not trying to face any of it, just trying to get through to herself, to what she'd been before, trying to be unchanged.

Her mother just wanted her to keep changing, to recognize the bend in the road and to keep taking it, not trying to straighten out what couldn't be straight again. It was one thing she had in common with Warner, that they both just wanted to go back. You couldn't of course go back, but there might be a way forward that allowed you in a sense to return. If that was possible. If that was reasonable. If that was *a good thing*.

It was impossible to know what was good. Was staying with him good? Was making him go? She'd be damned if she was moving to Atlanta. You had to start somewhere. Here.

"Mommy." It was Sophie clutching at her from the tub. "I think we're ready to get out." She showed her wrinkly fingers. Daniel was still playing happily. How long had she had them in there? Every time she thought of time she winced, as if unzipping a part of her head that was painful.

"All right. All right." She lifted Sophie first and wrapped her in a towel, sent her to change into pajamas. Daniel she pulled up onto a towel set on her shoulder, and carried into his room where she wrestled him onto the changing table and dried and strapped and snapped him into a night diaper and pajamas. Her first night home in nearly three weeks.

"Bedtime story," she called.

"Mommy," Sophie nearly shrieked. "Mommy, we haven't eaten dinner."

"Oh right." She'd sent Warner out for pizza.

"It's here," he shouted. "Already cut and cooled. You guys have been up there forever."

He sounded too cheerful, and again she winced. She didn't want to see him. Could she just send the kids down without her? Sullenly she hoisted Daniel on her hip and headed for the stairs.

"Hey." He was grinning shyly. "I got us a Mojo."

It was their favorite kind. "Great," she said.

The four of them sat at the table between the pass-through and the sofa and the bed. He'd laid new plastic sheeting under Daniel's high chair and he noticed that she noticed. Sophie ate slice after slice of a child's pizza, and the baby slurped a jar's worth of chicken and rice. Warner wolfed down his entire half of the Mojo, grimacing still from the frying pan. Her first piece grew cold on her plate. Her poor mother. Her only mother. It wasn't going to be as easy as all that. And who was he, anyway? Who were the kids? She couldn't wait for and yet she dreaded their bedtime. They'd be upstairs and she'd be alone with him and what would they say? What would they do? She could go up to bed, but she didn't want to. She didn't feel well enough to get out. She just wanted to be alone.

"Could you do me a favor?" she said, not even waiting for the kids to finish their dinner. "Could you just go out while I'm putting them to bed? For about three or four hours." He looked at her, nodding in a stunned, dutiful way. "That would really help."

When he was gone and the kids were asleep, she sat in the red stuffed chair by the sofa and put her feet up on the cof-fee table and thought about how great it was to be home, to be alone, to be unwatched and untied and unmonitored. She lay on the futon and looked up at the popcorn ceiling and felt the room swell around her. Home. She made herself micro-wave popcorn and poured a glass of wine and sat at the din-ing table leafing through a *Glamour* that had arrived in her absence. Did she love him? Did she love anybody? The phone rang and she let it ring and the machine picked up and she hoped for a hang-up but the voice began, a voice at once distant and familiar to her and she fought the impulse to reach for it and then did.

"Hello," she said with an awful taste in her mouth.

"So how are you?" her father said. "Were you trying to get me to hang up or something? When did you get out?"

"Today," she said. She ate popcorn in his ear to show she was still herself.

"Skull surgery, hunh? Do you feel any smarter?"

They both laughed thinly. She sipped some wine.

"Is that a chardonnay I hear?"

"Doctor's orders," she said.

"I bet."

She drank in silence.

"I'm sorry I didn't call earlier. Julie and I just got back."

"Did you have a good trip?" she tried to ask brightly.

"We could hop a flight down there tomorrow morning. No big deal."

"That's all right."

"Can you explain any of it to me? I mean, do you want to?"

She shook her head. "No."

"Warner left the first message. Your mom—surprise, surprise—left one or two." He was trying to sound upbeat, and he wasn't succeeding. "It all sounds pretty screwed up."

"Uh-hunh."

"Well. All your running off at the mouth and stuff, it's hard to get a word in. I think I'm going to have to come see you."

"*Not* a good idea," she said.

"Should I call back?"

"I'll call you." She felt so tired she didn't think she could speak. "Soon. I promise." She hung up.

So she shouldn't have answered the phone. So what else was new? He'd be back in two hours, hardly any space at all. Again she cringed at the thought of time. She thought of how in the newspaper they always counted down the days left in the year, as if people couldn't wait for it to end, how so much of time was spent counting it down, as if people couldn't wait for it to run out. Sometimes she couldn't wait to die. What peace that would be, to die. She should have just died. Everything would have been so much simpler for her. To be dead. Nonexistent. Not at rest, she didn't believe at rest. But just done. Her head seemed to throb with the wine. It wasn't self-pity. It was everyone's destiny. Even her mother would die. How soon? How soon.

She set the wineglass in the sink and finished the dishes, picked up the living room, turned off most of the lights. Upstairs she slipped into Daniel's room and pried off her clothes, lay on the bed next to the crib. There'd been nights when she'd watched him fall asleep, his eyes shutting in degrees, opening once, shutting down again like phases of the moon, his butt high and then settling. How even his feet slackened, his hands, the fullness of his cheek, his breathing slow and rich, luxurious. It was better, the not knowing. The absolute uncertainty. This much she knew.

Of course Warner had suspected and he'd asked her and she'd denied it. Of course he still kept it somewhere in his head, perhaps it was one of the things that drove him into what he had become. It had been a mistake. She could deny it as long as he asked. She could keep denying it because maybe it hadn't happened, maybe she'd only imagined it. Imagined that midnight walk up the stairs of the upside-down house in Somerville, after that last fight during the week of Sophie's birthday party, how he'd said never no way would he have a second, how desperate she'd felt, how enraged. They'd talked about children before they'd married, talked about how they'd wanted them—not just one, *them*—and like so many other times it had not held in his mind, and he was saying no, definitely no, absolutely no. In the kitchen she'd poured herself a glass of wine by the light of the open refrigerator, and then sat in the dark on the oatmeal sofa while below he'd slept. She'd wept, perhaps she'd slept, too, and cried in her sleep. She couldn't quite remember. She didn't *want to.* Then it was three or four, and she'd woken to the blurred image of Malcolm, Malcolm the listener who'd come out from the little guest room, patting her shoulder, telling her to wake up, it was only a dream, it would be okay, he and Claire knew how upset she was about the second child, they'd talked about it, they could help. Did she want to talk to Claire? She'd shaken her head. She'd felt still a little unclear from the wine, they'd drunk a lot that night and having that extra glass just a while ago had seemed to trigger it all.

Malcolm had gone into the kitchen and returned with a fresh glass of wine for each of them. They drank. She'd always admired him, but she didn't know him like she knew Claire. Now he talked about how much he liked playing in his jazz band, about the last piece he'd done in ceramics class. Another glass of wine? he asked. She nodded, and he seemed to come back before he'd even gone. I can help, he said, if you want me to. Fucking Warner, she said. Yeah, he agreed, fucking Warner. Claire says he's an asshole. Maybe he touched her. Do you want to? Is now a good time? Why do you think we're fighting about it, she nearly laughed. Now *is* the time. Now? *Now.* Now he was touching her, now she was touching him, practically clinically, practically medically. I can come fast, he might have said. Good, she could have murmured. Good. If it had happened, if she let herself believe it had happened, it *had* been fast. Soon she was downstairs again, sleeping. Sleeping till Warner woke her, at five, at five-thirty. Where were you, he said. Upstairs, sipping wine. I fell asleep. I love you, he said. I'm sorry. He'd reached over and begun the certain delicate assured moves that meant what they always meant—to her horror, to her triumph, to her relief. They'd done it. And again, despite his bitterness, the next afternoon while Malcolm and Claire took the kids to the playground for an hour. And then they'd fought, again, about having or not having one, about the money and the cost and the time and the energy and the exhaustion of it, and she swore that that was it, if it hadn't worked, she was done with it. He'd won. When she called him at the office to tell him otherwise, he said "Fuck!" and nearly hung up. At times, a moment here, a moment there, he'd asked her where the hell she'd been that night. He told her he suspected. Don't be stupid, she said. But he couldn't quite believe she'd gotten pregnant when they'd done it only twice.

When the baby came, he had all her looks, but Sophie's hair, Warner's hair. Are you sure, Warner had said. Don't be so insecure, she'd said. And whenever he brought it up, she offered that they could get a blood test. That would be too ridiculous, he admitted. But still he wondered. He loved that boy, but he couldn't help wondering. Where had she been that night. Upstairs, sipping wine, dozing. Maybe it hadn't happened. She couldn't tell anymore. The way you blurred what you knew to be true with what you wanted to be true, the mercy of denial. She'd never spoken a word of it to Malcolm, and Malcolm as if in the midst of some predesigned agreement or as if he knew the difference between dream and reality had never mentioned anything like it. She understood that sometimes the truths that were most essential to determine were also the truths that were inaccessible. And Warner loved Daniel, sucked him up with love, those cheeks—*What cheeks!* the doctor had said at delivery, and they hadn't yet lost their fullness, their roundness—those eyes, those forearms, those hands, those feet, those lips, that tender neck. Oh how he loved him, loved him up, this boy who might not be his.

Some stuff you just knew not to ask. You didn't say, Daddy, did you whack her. You didn't say, Mommy, is it all over now, is it all done. But you heard them talking, and you learned to wait. It was hard. He wanted to move. They'd already moved a lot. They'd have to promise her stuff if they moved. Cats or a dog. A bike. Where would they move? Are we moving, she did ask. Maybe, he'd said, and Mommy shushed him. Maybe wasn't a good idea with her, wasn't ever a good idea. She liked *to know.* Tell me as soon as you know, she told Daddy. Okay, he said. Sure. Absolutely. A word they both liked.

She was absolutely going to school every day. If they moved, she was absolutely going to get a cat. She would absolutely always have her own room. She was absolutely their little girl, and they absolutely loved her all the time always.

Spring came. It came in the winter, sometime in February, or very early March, and the crape myrtle bloomed Mommy said to the point of tackiness and the grass was green, almost a bright green as if it had been painted, and they went on weekends to the one big park with the duck-turd-pocked walkways around the big pond and bought feed from the quarter machines and she and Daniel fed the ducks till the quarters ran out. During the week Daddy sent letters to every place that Mommy could stand to think of living in, and

Mommy sent letters too because one job was not enough. As she understood it one job was absolutely not enough. Some weeks Daddy flew off for two or three days and returned tired and grumpy. Some weeks Mommy flew. When she came back, she was always happier. She said it refreshed her to be away. Daddy said that being away taught him to love them more, but it wore him out, although he really didn't work during the week otherwise. He cooked all the dinners—always noodles—and he made sure they didn't spend any money that they didn't have to.

One week both Mommy and Daddy had to go away together and this could really be the start of something new they said and Grandpa came down with Julie and they went to all the parks and playgrounds and Carowinds and did all the rides that she was by the rules allowed to go on and Daniel squawked and squawked because he couldn't go at all and her head spun and she didn't get sick even though Grandpa and Julie thought she would. But she ate and ate whatever she wanted and by the time Mommy and Daddy came back she hadn't pooped in a long time and they looked at her and they knew it.

"*Dad,*" Mommy told Grandpa.

"Hey," Grandpa said, "you can't force her to eat what she won't eat. But we had fun, didn't we?"

Grandpa and Julie left and for a long two days or three Mommy and Daddy made her take milk of magnesia and the food tasted different and the day she finally went was the day she learned that in three months they were moving to Pennsylvania.

"We're moving home," Daddy said.

"I thought we were home," she said.

"You'll get a cat," he said.

"I will!" she clapped.

"She will?" Mommy said.

He nodded. "I promised."

"You're really going?" Milicent looked both annoyed and confused as she tried to look at Megan as neutrally as possible. "I mean, honey, Pennsylvania has the second-worst economy in the country and North Carolina has the second best. Doesn't that tell you something?"

"We can get a house there for half the price." Megan recrossed her legs and sipped her coffee as they sat cozily in the back office of the new gallery.

"I guess I just can't believe you're going with *him*." Again Milicent tried not to look sour, but Megan could see it.

"It's a good move," she said. "He'd never get a job down here."

"I understand that."

The door gonged, and Megan stood. "It's him." She picked up her purse. "We're going to lunch."

"Well." Milicent lit a cigarette and stayed where she was. "Have a good one, dear."

He was waiting out in the atrium, looking natty and nervous in a summer sport coat.

"Ready?" he said.

They walked through the glass and marble quickly, the bankers due to descend in about three minutes for their lunches. At Carpe Diem they were given the odd table up in the window with their backs to the arriving crowd. She wondered how he felt being on a kind of display like this. She didn't care either way. Soon they were leaving, and she was thrilled. They both ordered fish and a glass of wine. He always used to make them order a whole bottle. She never drank at lunch. She couldn't help smiling at these minor changes. The wine came immediately, and she could see he was struggling to nurse it. That was all right. Behind her she could feel all the money, and it made her shiver.

"Nine more weeks," he said.

"I can't wait."

"I got a dozen more used boxes today. And two of those wardrobe things."

She smiled gratefully but didn't say a word. She preferred not to talk about the actual mechanics of anything. He was all mechanics, but lately he seemed to be learning at least not to talk about it.

"So," he said.

"So."

The salads arrived, and he concentrated on how much pepper the waitress was applying. He was being irritating today. She supposed he couldn't help it. Can't you help it? she wanted to say. She was no longer hungry, and the wine wasn't helping. What are we doing? she wanted to say. She made herself eat her salad. They hadn't been out alone together since November.

"It's been a long time between dates," she said.

"Yes." He drank more water, his third or fourth glass.

"You're nervous."

"Everything is so weird," he said quietly. "Sometimes I just want it to stop."

"Ahhh," she said.

He gulped his water. "You think we should see somebody?"

She looked at him; she knew what he meant, and she'd

seen enough people. She shook her head. "If you want," she said.

"Well, anyway." He shrugged, looking oddly relieved. "We're still together."

She ate her fish feeling the victory of that. They were still together. At least that was undeniable. At least they had that. Her mother didn't. Her father didn't—or he did, but it was the fourth time around for him. Everybody might think she was sick or stupid, but she knew better. She knew exactly what she had.

"Do you think we're staying together just for the sake of staying together?"

He would ask that. Sometimes he was so much like his mother, so literal and relentless, that it amazed her that she'd missed seeing these qualities in the first place.

"Maybe," she said. "What would *I* know about why people stay together?"

"Oh," he said.

She forced a smile. "This is some first date," she said.

Years ago, when his brother was getting anxious about his own impending wedding, Warner took a train to New York to try to help him. The wedding was in just six days, and they sat in the kitchen of the apartment his brother shared with his fiancée. I just think of all those women out there, his brother said. Is she really the one? Do I have to make this choice now? Maybe I should wait. It was all such a cliché that Warner practically yawned in his face. He was newly married himself, just one year before, and on their wedding day he'd been so scared that Megan had joked that he looked ready to jump. Marriage isn't about shutting yourself down, he told his brother, it's about opening yourself up. It's a great big wide huge field on which you can grow anything you want. His brother got married anyway.

These weeks Warner packed boxes and argued with movers and began to close on a house that Megan had flown up to find and picked out on her own. It was a luxury to be alone all day working with his hands and dickering on the phone. In the late afternoon he'd hunt down the children at their daycare and pre-school and drive in to pick up Megan. They tried not to talk too much. She was excited about the house. He'd seen pictures—it was redbrick and boxlike, with a mansard roof and an attached garage on a wraparound corner lot. They'd have to buy a lawn mower. The town was small, historic, fifteen miles above the Mason-Dixon line, and there weren't many choices. There were no private schools or magnet schools or special schools. There were no good, expensive restaurants and no gourmet food stores and no malls and no clothing stores and no bookstores. There were no cafés, no private tennis clubs, no imported car dealerships. There were jobs for both of them that paid as much as they had been making in January, before everything, and there was very little to spend it on and their house was so cheap that the monthly mortgage was going to be less than the rent at Crape Myrtle Hill. His board president was a man in his late fifties who slurred his words and trembled, and Megan's boss was a woman in her early fifties with perfect enunciation but still a hint of a tremor. Everybody they'd met during their interviews shook a little bit or stuttered in their speech. People said it was the copper in the plumbing or the river valley air or whatever might be drifting down from Three Mile Island. Sometimes Warner felt they were going to Pennsylvania to die. Each day he wrote out lists of all the things he was supposed to accomplish, and it made him happy just to draw a line through each one.

By mid-May the weather grew hot and cloying, and he ran the air-conditioning all the time. The children came back to him sweaty and red-faced, and Megan complained about having to move in the heat. Each morning he packed five or six boxes and when the pre-school term finished he had completed the kitchen and all the breakables in the living-dining-bed room and study-nursery. He pulled Daniel from daycare. In the mornings before the weather became unbearable he took the children to the pool across from the playground. Sophie paddled around in her swim ring. Daniel jumped from the edge, arms out, into him as he waited. Sometimes the boy intently ducked himself underwater, his whole round head submerged, and Warner would hoist him instantly up and Daniel gurgled the chlorine taste as if it were juice. They were crazy about the water. He took them again in the late afternoon. After picking up Megan in the evening he allowed himself a gin and tonic—what a real summer drink that felt like—while she noodled them through dinner and into bedtime. He found himself wishing that he never had to work again. He liked packing, doing dishes. He loved the sunburned, sunwashed feeling of nine o'clock, the children asleep, him in a pair of shorts and a T-shirt, Megan marveling at the great job that he was doing getting them ready for the move. He didn't want to move anymore—he just wanted to pack.

He was sitting on the sofa comparing mortgage rates when the phone rang. It was past ten o'clock. Megan was in her pajamas, and she looked at him quizzically. He had a feeling, he just had a feeling.

"Hello?" he said, unable to hide the dread.

"Warner?" It was his brother. "It's Ronald. I'm afraid—"

"Oh no." He shut his eyes and tried to see his father, see him smiling, see him glaring, see him walking to the refrigerator, standing over the sink with a piece of fruit in his hand. One summer he'd carved Warner an amulet out of soapstone. He still had that amulet.

"It's"—Ronald was crying, gulping into the phone—"it was a heart attack."

Warner nodded, knowing. What else could it have been?

"She died quickly. No pain—"

"She?"

"It's Mom, it's Mom, it's Mom." He was sobbing. "I can't talk right now. I'll call you back."

"What is it?" Megan was saying, as he stood in the blank kitchen still holding the phone. "What is it?"

He shook his head and tried to speak. Something like a growl emerged. He tried again, feeling the sides of his face begin to crumble, his mouth numb. Oh god, his brother was right. You couldn't speak, you could only nod and feel the way your head moved on your neck. The way the floor moved underfoot, moved you back from the kitchen to the oatmeal sofa, the indifferent white walls of the living-dining-bedroom. They hadn't spoken since January. His own mother.

"My mother." He swallowed, looking uncertainly at Megan as if just saying the words would take the floor out from under him.

"Your mom?" Megan's eyes huge, her hand moving to her mouth, she sitting with him on the sofa. "Your mom?" she said again.

"My mom," he said, his face wet and crumpled. "Oh my mom."

• • •

He slept but didn't sleep. He woke but didn't wake. At first light he began packing. He couldn't wear the old gray suit that had gotten him through the arraignment, but all he had otherwise were sport coats. His best shoes were his wedding shoes. She leafed through her dresses soundlessly, stole into Sophie's room and gathered clothes and books and toys. They loaded the dozing kids into the car, and he drove them through Charlotte and up the spine of North Carolina. Sophie woke past Statesville, and he let Megan tell her. By nine they reached Virginia, and Daniel was crying continuously. Warner didn't want to stop. At a Dunkin' Donuts still in the hills Megan toileted the children and changed them and bribed them with something sweet while he stood in the men's room cupping water to his face. His own mother. How he had failed her. How she had clung to her lap desk, her files, her month-lies and quarterlies, as if they could prolong her life, as if by never letting them go they would never let her go. How they had failed her. How everything had failed her. He remem-bered how she had stood on the living-room steps at her sixti-eth birthday party and announced to everyone by way of a toast that they all knew she considered her life a failure and her children were her only reward. She had said that. He'd been blushing furiously at her side, thinking, Don't do this, Don't do this. She'd done it anyway. He remembered how she'd slapped him around, how he'd slapped her just that once. How her kisses felt, how her face felt against his when they hugged. How her back felt, her arms, her hands. How once when he was seven or eight he'd seen a couple neck on television and he'd strode into the kitchen and tried it on his mother and she'd laughed "Warner!" and wiped it away with the back of her hand. All the crap. How his father was alone. How big and empty and full of junk the house that he'd grown up in was.

"Warner?" Megan had discreetly pushed open the door of the men's room and was looking at him as she held on to Daniel and Sophie peered around her hip. "We're ready, honey. We should probably go."

He just wanted to get there, to see and hear and understand that it was true, to be released into the world of grief so that he could just stop moving and allow whatever was going to happen to happen.

Coming in past the airport he thought Pittsburgh was smaller and meaner than he remembered or expected, as if it were clenching itself at his arrival. The route in took him alongside one of the rivers, across from the buildings that at night would be outlined by strings of lights but now, on a June afternoon at four o'clock, seemed only dusty and bland. The exit ramp off and down and under the overpass and the road up over the hill and the stoplight shushing him and the turn left, the turn right. The driveway filled with his brother's and sisters' colorful shining cars, the house shut and blunt against the heat. He stopped the car. It had been over a year since he'd been here. Home. Six, seven months since anyone had spoken to him. The kids pushing and climbing from the backseat, Megan herding them toward the porch, the front door. The door unlocked, Daniel and Sophie squeaking it open. The house inside, the dark blue and red paisley wallpaper, the cold air-conditioning, the colonial-style shaded lamps emblazened with open-winged black eagles, the house that was never any good at letting the light in, the dark-wood floor. The kitchen. Voices. There was Ronald, there was

Ronald's wife, there were Molly and her husband, Helen's husband. From the den came the song of a children's television show. "Dad's asleep," someone said. The children tearing off for the television. Everyone hugging. Half-nibbled food on platters lining the counter. Helen coming in, wiping her face. "I'm closing in on a casket," she said, looking at everybody but Warner, "we'll need to go see it." A few volunteers moving toward the door. Warner climbed the stairs to stand outside his father's bedroom, smiling tearfully at the resilient peacefulness of his snoring. He went into his own room, his old room, now stripped bare, an office with a computer and a filing cabinet and a stack of monthlies and last year's bound reports. The bed gone, a foldout sofa in its place. The old desk gone. The toy chest gone. He was gone, he was somewhere else. Megan's voice floated up, negotiating with one of his brothers-in-law where everyone could sleep. The house frantic, dead, confounded.

"Hello."

He reeled, turning. "Dad."

"I didn't know I told anyone to call you."

Warner shook his head, his lip trembling. "Ronald," he said.

"I guess some people always have to do the right thing."

"I guess so." He looked at the floor. He felt eight again. How he hated coming home.

"Your mother." He took a step into the room, stopped, seemed to try to shrug off the rippling in his creased face. "You hurt . . . your mother . . . very much." He refused to cover his face, glowering and teary.

Warner nodded, still trying to find something to say, if he could say anything.

"She," his father's voice caving to an animal, throaty rawness, "she . . . loved you . . . so much." He had made it across the room, and now it looked as if he might pull back his white fist with whatever he had left and deliver something final and crushing.

"Go ahead," Warner heard himself, nearly beginning to shriek. "Go ahead! As if that will solve anything." Again he was an eleven-year-old standing in this room, his mother's face pushing at him, pushing, pushing, saying *Go ahead hit me, Go ahead hit me* tears running down her cheeks, her eyes puffy and brimming and him pulling back and opening his hand and swinging just the once, just the once, with enough force to stain her skin from her face to her neck. "As if that's all you all think I'm capable of." He *was* screaming, the sound of his voice stunning and propelling him, as if he couldn't get the words out fast enough. "As if I really did park the car in the lot with the children asleep and leave them in the car *like that.* As if I really did sneak into that gallery and tiptoe up behind her and grab that hammer just lying there on the floor *like some kind of invitation* and whack her whack her whack her as hard as I fucking could and leave her in her blood on the carpet and tiptoe back out of there and drive the fuck away with the kids still asleep in the car. As if that were really possible. As if I really could fucking do what you all think I'm capable of doing. Well fuck you, just fuck you." He was shrieking. "Just fuck all of you. Fuck this whole family. And fuck me fucking too."

"Honey." It was Megan, Daniel clinging to her knees, her clinging to him. "Honey, it's me. Look at me, honey." She took him in her arms, and the baby seemed to take him too, take him and hold him. "It's all right. It's all right."

208

"Everyone just take it easy. Just take it easy." That was Ronald, lawyerly, who hadn't after all gone to help pick out the casket. He stood beside his father, now slumped on the arm of an overstuffed chair, and patted his shoulder.

"We're okay," Megan said so slowly, so softly, that everyone couldn't help but hear her, "we'll be okay."

"Of course we'll be okay," Ronald said. "Everything will be fine."

"Yes," she was saying to Warner. She touched him, touched the collar of his shirt, just touched him. "Yes." Her head melted into his chest. How long had it been? Months and months. "We're going to be fine." The baby tight against his knees. His old room tight with all the people. His chest tight with all of them.

She held one of his hands and turned it over, looked at the fingers, how pale and impractical they were. She swallowed whatever it was that she thought she could think of saying.

On the foldout sofa in his old room they listened to Daniel in his port-a-crib squirming beside them. Sometimes he gave little yelps. It was one o'clock, two o'clock, two-thirty.

"I wish he'd just wake up and we could get it over with," Megan murmured into Warner's ear. He nodded. "You could go sleep downstairs if you wanted." A sofa was free in the living room. He shook his head. One summer night when he was fifteen he'd slept on that sofa because the upstairs had been hot, and in the morning his mother had told him that it wasn't good for the good furniture to be slept on. The den had people and all the rooms upstairs had people and he didn't want to go sit in the kitchen. He didn't mind lying there listening to the baby try to sleep. He liked how the short yelps made holes in the dark. For the first time in a long time he liked being in his room, maybe because it wasn't his room anymore. He liked being awake, hovering above sleep, her hovering beside him, Sophie with two of her cousins next door in Helen's old bedroom. The big empty house so filled. Sometimes he hoped that his father would sell it and sometimes he hoped that he wouldn't, the way that you could have years of debate in just an hour or two of sleeplessness.

"What are you thinking about?" she whispered. It was clear that she was trying to wake the baby and get it over with.

"Nothing," he barely said.

"I was thinking," she whispered. "I was thinking that the hammer wasn't on the floor."

"Well how the fuck should I know where it was?" he said aloud, startling them both.

"Huck," Daniel said. Then squealed and rolled and flattened himself again in the crib. They waited. He appeared to sleep.

"It was on the table," she whispered. "You didn't do it."

"Of course I didn't do it. Can we just fucking forget about it?"

"You didn't do it," she whispered again.

He made himself roll away from her even though he didn't want to. They could live in guilt or they could live in suspicion or they could live another way. He wanted the other way.

"I love you," she said softly.

"Me, too," he said.

For a long time she stared at his back, then shut her eyes

against the rustle of the baby. In a week no one could know that their Crape Myrtle Hill living room had also served as a dining room and master bedroom, that their nursery was also the study and the dressing room, that they had pushed and jammed themselves into every available foot of space, and still they hadn't fit.

Aftermath

*T*he Munchie Mouse at the Arboretum strip mall had four birthdays going at once, and Warner was obligated to stand with the other fathers beside the checker at the door and welcome whoever came for Sophie's party. They'd invited the entire Full Day Family except for the teachers, but only half of the kids' parents had RSVP'd. Megan had called and gotten a host of answering machines and uncertain voices. They had no idea how many people to expect.

He counted less than a dozen, their parents giving him the once-over as they dropped them at the entrance. "Hello," he kept saying, "hello. Sophie's party is right this way." The children eyed him warily as they passed, as if they'd been warned. But it was Munchie Mouse, and you couldn't take a kid home unless your wrist tags matched. They were safe.

The party itself was in a yellow room with an orange-curtained stage beyond the pinball-duckpin-junglerama area. Megan had arranged a bag of favors at each setting, and easily she sat the kids at their places and had them give the waiter their drink orders. Three large pizzas arrived, and Warner divided them onto paper plates and handed them around and dutifully the children began to eat. In five minutes they were done and they raced en masse to the games with rolls of tokens clutched in their hands. Daniel stumbled after them.

"This is," Megan said, as she and Warner brought up the rear along a path of brown carpet littered with wrappers and crusts, "the tackiest thing I have ever done."

"It's what she wanted," he said.

"Like the cat. You never asked me, Warner."

"It was in the heat of the moment," he said.

The children tangled with all the other kids from all the other parties while he and Megan tried to keep track of and placate Daniel who was alternately being coddled and bullied by Sophie's friends. His little pockets bulged with tokens that kept dribbling out, and he wasn't tall enough to reach most of the coin slots. Soon he was sitting on the floor with his legs sprawled out in front, bawling. Warner took him to the junior game room, but all he wanted was to be with *sisser* and her buddies in the big room.

"Sophie Lutz's party," Megan announced, over the gongs and hoots and whistles and pops and musical jangle of the video battles and game-room sound track. "Cake and present time."

They swept and dragged the kids back to their table.

"Cake time," Megan told the waiter.

Under his orange and yellow Munchie Mouse hat he nodded sagely and blew a whistle with three short blasts. Five other wait staff came running, the orange curtain opened, and a six-foot mouse in a sweater vest strolled to the center of the stage and started to croon into a cordless microphone a personalized rock-and-roll "Happy Birthday" while the wait staff clapped to the beat and the mouse descended the stairs to stand beside Sophie, her eyes bright with ecstacy. On the last note the mouse opened his furry arms and Sophie rushed into them and buried her face in his belly. The mouse waved to the rest of the children, his hand flat up to ensure they kept their distance, paused for a few photographs from Megan, extricated himself from the birthday hug, and with an unexpected dignity returned up the stairs and was swallowed by the closing orange curtain. The children clapped and whistled and danced and blew on their party horns.

There were still the presents and another hour of gaming to get through, and then they had to rush home and incorporate all the loot into the final frantic packing. But Sophie was happy, her friends were happy, Daniel hopped with glee, and when Megan and Warner turned to each other, they shared a look of stunned recognition. He could not tell whether they were seeing something about themselves or Charlotte, or whether it was simply because soon they would escape.

She cut the cake, and he passed the slices around, and the children nibbled while they watched as Sophie began to open her presents, awaiting their release to the game room.

"Say thank you," Warner quietly prompted at every unwrapping. "Say thank you."

There were three Barbies and a few craft sets and a board game that he had also played as a kid, where you took a pair of metal-tipped tweezers and tried to remove various organs and bones from their rigged wells in an electric body and if you stumbled or misstepped the red bulb of the nose flashed and the game board buzzed.

"I used to love that game," he told all the kids.

"It's too easy," one of the bigger boys said. "I win that game all the time."

Soon the presents were done, and they followed the kids back to the game room. Within a miniature jalopy Sophie had her picture taken one by one with all the girls from her class. None of the boys would do it. The pictures cranked out from a slot in the machine and were on thermal paper and instantly curled. Warner collected them and folded them carefully into his pocket. The girls who wanted Sophie's picture then had her join them on the jalopy. Megan and Daniel were lost somewhere in the junglerama. A few of the boys ran out of tokens, and Warner bought them more. Eventually the parents returned, and called for their children from the entrance. Sophie said her good-byes as the parents waited at a distance. While Megan paid the bill Daniel slept on Warner's shoulder.

On the way to the car, pushing a shopping cart filled with the presents, Megan elbowed Warner and pointed and laughed. Even through the oppressive heat of the tarry parking lot he could see what she meant. In the road grime on the undented side of the Honda someone had written, "Good Luck."

After the movers had emptied their truck and left them in their own home, they stood in the kitchen, sweaty and smiling. It wasn't yet noon; they'd survived the drive the day before, the night at the cheap hotel, the early morning with the sellers and the lawyers in the old stuffy office off the square of their new town. Everything had come back to them. Nothing had gone astray in the five hundred miles. They were moved.

Their house was bright, with large windows everywhere, red carpeted stairs and hallways for the children to make a racket on, blond-wood floors in all the rooms. Everyone had their own bedroom, the kids had their own bathroom with a tub. In the basement was a tacky long-ignored bar with waist-high vinyl stools mounted in the floor. It was just as Megan had said. It was wonderful.

"Well," she said, still grinning. She couldn't seem to stop. It was at least twice as big as the town house at Crape Myrtle Hill and five times as bright. "You could take the kids somewhere, and I could start unpacking."

"Children?" he called, loving the sound of the word. He dimly remembered passing orchards where you could pick your own fruit not far from town, near the Maryland border. "Let's go find some blueberries!"

"Blueberries?" Sophie came running. He ran to the stairs in time to catch Daniel taking them one step at a time on his butt. "I *love* blueberries."

They kissed Megan good-bye, trundled through the breezeway, and disappeared into the garage. A garage! A breezeway! A home! It really was some kind of town.

From the kitchen she watched them back carefully into the street. How oddly happy everyone looked. It might be the happiest they'd ever been. She felt strangely terrified. She got out the Swiss Army knife and went to the first kitchen box, cut it open, felt her way in through the Styrofoam chips and bubble wrap. Nothing apparently broken. She'd kept an eye on the movers. They hadn't been especially careful, but they hadn't been careless either.

It struck her, unpacking that first box in the almost too-bright kitchen, stopping to pull down the venetian blind over the large bay window, it struck her for the sixtieth or seventieth time that the week before in Pittsburgh when he'd screamed and shouted about the hammer, how he'd attached "invitation" to it—it lay on the floor *like some kind of invitation*—and in a way the invitation had been to her and she had taken it. She could turn it around in her mind as many times as she wished—the terrible emotion of the moment, the deliberate phrase of his admission of where he thought the hammer had been, the fact in question that could have been known even by those who didn't know—and still she had accepted his invitation. What was the truth anyway? It seemed to her that the truth became hidden behind a scaffolding so delicate and elaborate and entwined—a scaffolding constructed between oneself and the other and between the two of you and the world—that to try to remove it was to risk discovering that the truth could not actually exist apart from it. Perhaps she was just being cynical. Perhaps she was just being perceptive. It was a fine line, and she'd watched him for twelve years straddle it himself, the most negative person she had ever known. She brought out the espresso machine and set it on the counter. It, coupled with the house, made her feel almost embarrassingly rich. Across the street, behind the elementary school that Sophie would attend, was a shopping center sunk in an asphalt valley, half of its windows boarded shut, offering only a discount supermarket and an optometrist's office. The Realtor had told her that a flood last summer had wiped out a drugstore, a video store, a women's boutique, and an office supply store. There were no plans to reoccupy the space. It was good for the property values, she had observed to Megan, to keep the center half shut. It would cut down on the street traffic. Perhaps eventually even the school would close, but that was years into the future.

Megan wiped clean the espresso machine and set it on the corner of the expansive kitchen counter, between the stove and the sink. She felt uncertain, unpacking into so much space. For the first time since they'd been living together there wouldn't be a question of what to unpack and what to keep in storage. The challenge, instead, would be to fill all the cabinets. Even the wedding china could come out, and she hadn't seen that since Somerville. They used to have mock discussions about whether its trim was red brick or deep orange. The pattern was Colorado. As graduate students they once had gone camping in Colorado, at the Frying Pan River. One night they'd driven into Aspen and tentatively entered its trendiest restaurant under recurring patterns of a neon-lit moon. They were seated, and for twenty minutes they waited. Finally Warner had stood and gone to the server station and asked for service. The few staff had looked him up and down and one waitress with bright red lipstick and a black Gucci skirt had said something and he'd returned red-faced to the table. "What'd she say?" Megan asked, as he led them from the restaurant, pocketing a logoed ashtray on the way. "She said," he remarked as dryly as he could, "'*Maybe.*'" They'd eaten at a bar where one of the patrons discovered a baby rat in a can of beer he was drinking, and a local TV news team almost instantly converged. Was it planted or was it real? It was hard to believe that guy. He was muddy and fat with a beard down his belly so snarled the rat could have come from there. They wanted to believe him, and besides they got to drink free the rest of the night. On the way back to the campground along the swirl of road by the river they'd been nearly sideswiped by a car, which then crunched over a raccoon. They stopped and watched it struggling in its own heap. It slunk to the side of the road. "Thank god," she said. "I don't think I could have moved it." "Neither could I," he admitted. Who was to say why some people stayed together and some didn't? Who was to say there was any necessary truth? She finished unwrapping the china and set it in his grandmother's antique bar, latched it shut

Charlotte

.7 rich & poor

20-1 Boom town
(envy)

22 six figures

36 carpet happy

65 Charlotte dirt

83 Myers Park

104 & Elizabeth

.132 To hell with
Myers Park

against the children, then climbed the wide red stairs to begin on their rooms.

By the time Warner reached the Mason-Dixon line Daniel's head slumped peacefully against the wing of his car seat and Sophie's eyes were shut, their faces composed and sealed by sleep. His brother-in-law had once told him that having kids was so wild and astonishing because they were so dependent on you, and he had mumbled assent even though he was not sure he agreed. At first it was wild because of the loss of control, that you gave up so much of your life to them, that some days you could barely make it to the refrigerator or the bathroom because their demand was so constant. And then maybe it was wild because of how you could sense they loved you and trusted you unconditionally; that even if they fought or tried to undermine you, they still wanted you. Now he couldn't quite see why it was wild, but he knew it was. Maybe the why didn't matter. Maybe you could never know the why. Maybe it was better just to stop asking. He was a parent, and that gave him such a fullness and focus, not only about them but about him, about what he wanted, about what he had. Those first weeks after Sophie was born, he had felt that the three of them were on a great ship together, just like the ship that he and Megan had been on, but this ship drifted taller in the water and felt large enough to cross an ocean, and this ship sailed night and day. Occasionally he or Megan would cast out for diapers or food, but in those first weeks that was the only reason why one of them ever left the other two. Then his leave had ended, and every day he left for work, and he lost his sense of the ship. He didn't know if the ship was home or work or going out with his buddies to a bar or if there was a ship. Then Megan returned to her job, and a baby-sitter came to the apartment, and sometimes Sophie was dropped at daycare, and he was certain that home was not a ship. In Boston when Daniel came, Sophie kept going to school, and it was never always just the four of them. Now at least, with school close by, with their work close by, with evenings and weekends, with the simple fact that he even got to live with them, he could feel the ship. The ship was the car, the ship was the house, the ship was wherever and whenever they were. He wished Megan could have come with them for blueberries.

As a child he had always been terribly homesick whenever he'd been sent away to camp. He wrote letters to his parents begging them to come get him. When they refused, he wrote "You bitch" to his mother, and said he would slash his wrists or hurt her. He checked himself into the infirmary and refused to leave. They finally came for him. Two summers this happened, and during the school year he felt the loss of home so much that often his mother or father came and sat in the lobby just to keep him attending class, and on the eve of the third summer, when his mother told him how he needed to grow up, how he disgusted her, he hit her. And then he understood. He understood that if he could not be with her always, he would just have to hate her. He hated her because he could not be with her all the time, and so he made sure he was with her less and less. He had no time for her, and when he was with her he had no patience.

It was too easy to see—that he struck whenever he was wounded. That it wasn't about money and it wasn't about work. It was about love and how work and money and just living ate into any warmth and solace you could find. He was sorry about his mother. He was sorry about Megan. He was sorry about Daniel and Sophie. But he would stop being fucking sorry about himself. He would have to take the wounds as they came.

In Catoctin at the orchard he unbuckled the sleeping children, loaded Daniel on his shoulder, and led Sophie by his free hand to a clapboard stall where they were given a two-pound plastic bucket.

"Over here," a woman called to him out from one of the rows of low leafy bushes. "Here's good." She pointed him past groups of quiet pickers to a stretch of bushes ten yards in front of her. "Now don't pick the green berries," she added, almost scolding. "We still have to charge you for them and they won't ever turn and that'll be a waste."

In an overcast damp stillness they stood before the bushes pocked with fruit. He held the bucket for them.

"Okay," he said softly. He took Daniel's hand and led him to a blueberry. "Pick the blue one, the dark one. Okay. Not the green ones."

"'Kay," Daniel said. "Boo."

"Look, Daddy." Sophie showed him several plump blueberries. "Right?"

"Right." He gestured with a flattened downturned hand to tell her to keep her voice low. She shrugged but nodded.

The sun popped out, and he wished he'd put lotion on them. At least in the silence they were steadily filling the bucket. Soon he'd get them back to the car, back on the road. He had some lollipops in his pocket for the ride, and the air-conditioning was working. The hills between them and home were so green they looked blue, and the road back was bare and bleached. There were sheep and horses, and just across the state line there was a deep-red barn; his father had taught him that most barns were red because it was the cheapest paint color that could be kept relatively clean. Sometimes his father knew a lot, and Warner wished he could remember that more often.

"Hey," Sophie cried piercingly. "Hey, Daddy!"

"What?" he said. "What is it?"

"Look."

Daniel was picking all the berries he could get his hands on and slapping them in the bucket. Not too many were blue.

"They're *green*," Sophie whined loudly.

"It's okay, honey, it's okay." He tried to smile reassuringly as he felt the other pickers and the two women who ran the orchard eyeing them through the broken calm.

"But Daddy, we'll get charged for them and they'll never turn and we won't be able to eat them and they'll waste." She frowned and glared at her brother.

"Een," Daniel was crowing. "Ween!" He threw more and more green berries in, and they thwacked against the sides like pellets.

"Daddy!"

"Really, Sophie," Warner said gently, and held her wrist as she stared at him questioningly, "it's not a big deal."